H. A. Guerber

Legends of Switzerland

H. A. Guerber

Legends of Switzerland

ISBN/EAN: 9783337151157

Printed in Europe, USA, Canada, Australia, Japan

Cover: Foto ©Andreas Hilbeck / pixelio.de

More available books at **www.hansebooks.com**

LEGENDS

OF

SWITZERLAND

BY

H. A. GUERBER

WITH ILLUSTRATIONS

NEW YORK
DODD, MEAD AND COMPANY
1909

DEDICATED

TO

SWITZERLAND

IN GRATEFUL MEMORY OF HAPPY SUMMERS SPENT
WITHIN ITS BORDERS

PREFACE

ASIDE from the picturesque, historical, and geological interest connected with a journey in Switzerland, that country also boasts of a rich fund of legends, delightfully characteristic of the people at whose firesides they have been told for centuries.

The grand scenery, terrific storms, sudden earthquakes, landslides and avalanches, together with the barbaric invasions and fierce wars which have swept over it for thousands of years, have all left their indelible stamp, not only upon the face of nature, but also in the imagination and folklore of the people.

In varying keys, and touching upon many chords and themes, these legends refer to saints and to sinners, to heathen gods, giants, ghosts, dwarfs, Devil, and fairies, as well as to kings and queens, knights and ladies, monks and nuns, besides dwelling particularly upon shepherds, pastures, cattle, and game.

The rustic crudity of some of these tales, the mediæval halo of romance around others, added to the poetic subtle charms of a few, have been rendered as faithfully as possible, to enable the reader to gain a nearer insight into the life and thoughts of the sturdy race which has established the most lasting republic in modern Europe.

Life-long familiarity with the official languages, some knowledge of the peculiar dialects, together with prolonged sojourns in the country, and diligent study of its principal works on national folklore, have enabled the writer to collect these legends, some of which are now laid before the English-speaking public for the first time.

Trusting they may enhance the pleasure of a trip to Switzerland for all those who have the good fortune to enjoy one, remind former travellers of matchless scenes, and amuse and interest even stay-at-homes, this book is sent out into the world with the sincere hope that it may meet with a kindly welcome.

CONTENTS

ILLUSTRATIONS

Legends of Switzerland

LEGENDS OF GENEVA

THE crescent-shaped Leman, or Lake of Geneva, the largest and bluest of all the Swiss lakes, has been sung by all the poets and praised by every writer who has had the good fortune to behold it in its native splendour.

The fertile slopes on the northern bank, the charming resorts and drives to the east and south, and the glorious view of Mont Blanc, in Savoy, as seen from Geneva itself, bewitch all those who are privileged to enjoy them. Countless steamboats and sailboats are constantly plying to and fro over the lake, and stopping at picturesque points along the shore, whence delightful excursions can be made either among rich pastures, orchards, and vineyards, or up into the mountains from which, rippling and roaring, torrents and streams pour down to fill the basin of this beautiful lake. The most picturesque craft on the Lake of Geneva are

the lateen-sailed market-boats, hovering like
birds over waters whose colour reminds one of
the Mediterranean, the only other body of
water in Europe where such vessels are frequently seen.

A legend claims that in olden times a fairy
boat of this peculiar shape was often seen flitting from point to point along the shores of
Lake Leman. Its sails catching every gleam
of golden light, it shone like the face of the
new moon in a summer sky. Drawn by eight
large snow-white swans, it glided gently over
the waters, to the song both weird and sweet
of these graceful birds, accompanied by the
thrilling chords of a harp touched by the invisible fingers of the Spirit of the Winds.

Standing by the mast of this ship, was a tall
woman of dazzling beauty, whose golden locks
streamed out in the breeze, while the sunset
flush on the snow-mountains seemed no more
delicate than the bloom on her dainty cheeks.
Clad in flowing robes of purest white, she stood
there, smiling gently at countless winged and
chubby sprites, hovering around her like butterflies about a rose, and scattering handfuls of
flowers and fruit at her feet.

It is said that wherever the fairy ship touched
the shore, the soil bore flowers and fruit in

LAKE OF GENEVA, WITH DENT DU MIDI.

abundance, and any one who was so fortunate as to catch a glimpse of the lucky vessel was sure of the fulfilment of any desire, expressed or unexpressed. Even when buried so deep in the hidden recesses of the heart that the owner was scarcely conscious of its existence. the fairy's melting blue eyes were sure to discover this wish, and her heart was so tender that, once discovered, she could not but grant it.

The fairy skiff of Lake Geneva haunted its shores for many years, and might still be seen there, had not the giant swans been frightened away by the puffing and snorting steamboats which furrow the blue waves. None but the oldest inhabitants ever mention this ship, of which they caught fleeting glimpses in their early youth. when they sat by the lakeside during the long moonlight nights. in hopes of securing the realization of their dearest hopes.

But the luck-ship figures not only in the tales told by the peasants around the fireside during the long winter evenings ; it is also often seen in effigy upon Genevan holiday and birthday cards. Then " Good Luck," or " Happy New Year," is inscribed across the wing-like lateen sails. and such a card is supposed to bring the happy recipient as much good fortune as an actual glimpse of the swan-drawn vessel of mythic fame.

An interesting old legend is connected with the church of Ste. Marie Madeleine in Geneva, and with a local yearly festival celebrated there on the twenty-second of July.

In the days when the Madeleine church was founded, Geneva, after having been the main stronghold of the Allobroges before Christ, and a Roman camp from the days of Cæsar until the fifth century, was the capital of a Burgundian kingdom. The Christians in that part of the country, desirous of building a church where they could worship God, selected a site just outside of the city fortifications, and then began to solicit contributions on all sides.

In those days there dwelt in Geneva a very good and pious girl, noted far and wide for her deftness in spinning, and for the unusual beauty and fineness of her thread. As soon as this virtuous maiden heard that funds were needed for a church to be dedicated to her patron saint, she made a solemn vow to consecrate to that good purpose all the thread she could spin, and immediately set to work.

From early morn until far into the night, Madeleine now spun on unweariedly, selling skein after skein of thread to purchase stones and mortar for the new building. As is always the case, the zeal and gifts of many of the

Christians soon ebbed, but Madeleine twirled her distaff faster and faster, working without respite day after day, to make up for all deficiencies.

The workmen, who contributed their labour, soon depended upon her alone for materials, and fearing lest her strength or courage should fail before the church was finished, they called out to her every time they passed her house to keep up a good heart and work on. This cry, —

> "Tiens bon, Marie Madeleine,
> Tiens bon, Marie Madelon!"

was taken up by all the Christians in town, and now forms the refrain of a song sung at Geneva's yearly festival.

Thus encouraged, Marie Madeleine went on spinning until the building was completed, and as most of the stones were purchased with the proceeds of her industry, the workmen carved spindles and spinning-wheels all over the church. On the festival of Ste. Marie Madeleine, illuminations and processions are the order of the day in Geneva, and the statue of a spinner is carried along all the principal streets of the town, to the rhythmic chant of the old distich, which commemorates alike the maiden's piety and her extreme diligence.

LEGENDS OF VAUD AND VALAIS

LATE in the spring, when the grazing down in the valley is pretty well exhausted, farmers in Switzerland are wont to drive their cows up to the mountain pastures, which by this time are all covered with luxuriant grass and gemmed with dainty wild-flowers. The day set for the departure of the cattle is always a gala day. The people, dressed in their Sunday best, assemble in the villages through which the herds must pass, to exchange merry jests with the herdsmen, bid them God speed, and admire the fat sleek cows, wearing around their necks bells of different sizes and varying tones.

The head herdsman proudly walks in front of his cattle, wearing a bunch of gay ribbons or of fresh flowers in his hat or cap. His blue cloth coat, with its short sleeves, sets off a dazzlingly white shirt of coarse linen, and his costume is completed by knee-breeches, thick woollen stockings, and shoes whose soles are elaborately studded with bright nails. This man carries a bag full of salt, and an umbrella slung across his back ; and from time to time, as he strides joyfully ahead of the herd, he offers a handful of salt to the foremost cows. Leaning on his stout staff, he sturdily climbs the mountain, giving vent to those long-drawn musical cries known as " huchées " or " jodels," according to the section of the country in which they are heard.

Close behind the herdsman comes the bull, with a ring in his nose, or a fine cow, the queen and leader of the cattle. Conscious of the honour of wearing the largest and deepest-toned bell, this animal steps proudly along, tossing a shapely head decked with bunches of bright flowers on either horn, and between them rests the milking-stool, a sign of particular distinction.

Cow after cow slowly files past, greeted by calls and loving pats from proud owners, and amid the tinkling of bells, the trample of hoofs, the lowing of kine, and the cheers of the people sound the resonant cracks of the herdsmen's whips, which they snap incessantly to show their proficiency in that greatly admired branch of their calling.

The sight of such a herd going up the mountain invariably reminds the old people of happy summers long gone by, and while sitting on the benches in front of their stone or wooden houses

at twilight, they entertain the younger generation with reminiscences of the joyful past, and
a regretful sigh always heaves their aged breasts
when they finally mention the Golden Age of
Switzerland.

According to tradition, this was the time
when none of the mountains — not even the
highest — were ever veiled in cold mists, or
covered with ice and snow.   Neither were
there any barren and rocky heights such as we
see now.   Luxuriant grass grew all the way up
the steepest slopes, carpeting even the topmost
ridges, and the climate was so genial that
cattle dotted the hillside pastures during nine
or ten months of the year.   The cows were
then far larger and fatter than any we see now,
and their milk was so abundant that they were
milked thrice a day into huge ponds, or tanks,
where the herdsmen went about in skiffs to do
the skimming.

One of these men is said to have once lost
his balance and fallen head first into a lacteal
lake, but although his mourning companions
diligently sought for his corpse, and even
dredged that huge natural milkpan, they could
find no trace of him.   When churning-day came
round, however, and the big vats of thick cream
were poured into a churn as large and tall as a

THE MIGRATION OF THE HERDS.

castle tower, the dead man was suddenly discovered imbedded like a fly in the thick cream. The dairymen and milkmaids then mournfully laid his corpse to rest in a huge cave, lined with honeycombs so tall and massive that none was smaller than the city gates.

Such was the prosperity of all the farmers in the Cantons of Vaud and Valais, that their men used goat cheeses (*tommes*) instead of quoits for their daily games, and on Sundays played bowls with huge balls of the sweetest, hardest, yellowest butter that has ever been made. The fruit trees were as productive as the pastures ; the grapes, for instance, being so large and juicy that faucets had to be inserted in each grape to draw off the juice, while the pears were so fine and heavy that their stems had to be severed by means of a double hand-saw when came time to pick them.

The Golden Age of the Alps did not last long, however, for the unparalleled prosperity the people enjoyed filled their hearts with such inordinate pride that they became very insolent, and thereby called down the wrath of heaven upon their guilty heads. The brutality and avarice which they displayed was punished by earthquakes, storms, and landslides, which ruined their finest pastures, and by sudden and unwelcome changes in the temperature. Dense fogs swept over the mountains, and there were long and heavy snow-falls which swathed the mountains in a permanent casing of ice and snow. The summer season became far briefer than in the past, and fields and pastures much less productive. Cattle and fruit therefore soon dwindled down to their present comparatively small proportions, and unlimited plenty no longer reigned in the land.

In the Golden Age the country boasted of a few very large but quite benevolent giants. They roamed about at will, striding over mountains and forests, which seemed to them no larger than mole hills and tiny shrubs. The best known of these giants was Gargantua, renowned alike for his athletic proportions and for his childlike spirit. He was so huge that when he sat down to rest upon Mont Blanc, Monte Rosa, or some other large mountain, his legs hung down on either side until his feet rested comfortably in the valleys. Sometimes, when indulging in a brief noonday nap, he used one of these peaks as pillow for his huge and sleepy head. His thick white beard and hair, falling around him on all sides, then gave these heights somewhat the same aspect they have now, with their fields of snow and rivers

of ice. The sunken orbits of the giant's eyes
and his wide-open mouth looked like valleys
and crevasses, while his nostrils could be mistaken for deep and dark caves, and his ruddy
cheeks for great patches of red rock peeping
out among the snows.

When the weather was warm, Gargantua's
breath seemed like the mist hovering on the
mountain tops ; but when the temperature fell,
it rapidly congealed, spreading like a dense fog
all over the country. His gentlest snores are
said to have sounded like the distant rumble of
thunder, or the crash of avalanches ; and when
he stretched himself after a siesta, the whole
country was shaken as by a violent earthquake.

Once, while the giant lay asleep, his head
resting against a mountain, a large flock of
sheep scrambled up over his prostrate form,
and began to thread their way through his
tangled hair and beard in quest of pasture.
Awakened by a slight tickling sensation, the
giant half opened his sleepy eyes. The sight
of a host of little white creatures crawling around
in his beard so angered him, that he took them
up one by one between his thumb and index,
and crushed and threw them away, thinking
they were vermin.

During another nap a large herd of cows

strayed into the giant's wide-open mouth, which they mistook for a cave. Their presence there, however, occasioned a prodigious coughing-fit, in the course of which the cows were ejected with such force that they flew through miles of space and landed in another country!

As simple and innocent as he was large, Gargantua delighted in playing in the dirt. To amuse himself, he hollowed out the Rhône valley, and scooped out a basin for the Lake of Geneva. There the marks of his fingers can still be seen, for having no other tools he freely used those nature provides, flinging handfuls of earth and stones on either side of him, or into a rude basket made of wattled pine-trees which he carried on his back.

At one time Gargantua elected to build a fine sand-heap, and carried load after load of dirt and stones to a point southeast of the present city of Geneva. There he dumped them one after another, and as the heap increased in size after each basketful, he gleefully cried: " Ça lève, ça lève!" (It is rising, it is rising!) This cry was overheard by the people in the neighbourhood, who ever after used it as a name for that mountain, changing the orthography to Salève.

Gargantua sometimes threw huge rocks

around him in sport, or in petulant fits of anger, punched holes in and through the mountains, and dug out fistfuls of earth here and there to fashion his mud pies. He also liked to make gullies for the streams which trickled down the mountains. Once, while scratching out the Illiez valley he forgot the burden on his back and stooped to drink from the Rhône, which seemed to him like a mere rill. By some mischance, however, he stubbed his big toe against the rocks of St. Triphon, and fell sprawling along the valley, spilling part of the dirt out of his basket. The simple fellow, amazed at this accident, picked himself up gravely and uttered the local substitute for " My goodness ! " (Eh Monteh !). This exclamation was thereafter used by the natives to designate a mound of earth now covered with oak forests and known as Monthey.

In his wrath at having tripped and broken the straps fastening his basket to his back, Gargantua gave his burden an ill-tempered kick, which sent it flying some distance further on, where it dumped the rest of its contents. This heap of dirt formed the picturesque eminence on whose wooded heights the ruined tower of Duin now stands.

A similar accident occurring when the giant

once tried to quench his thirst in the Sarine, is the alleged origin of the hill upon which rises the church of Château d'Oex. On another occasion, resting one foot upon the top of the Berra and the other upon the Gibloux, Gargantua bent down and took a draught from the Sarine, which drained it so dry that not a drop of water flowed along its bed for three whole days. During that time one legend claims that the giant laid the foundation for the bridge at Pont-la-Ville, near Fribourg, but another ascribes that construction to his Satanic Majesty in person.

Gargantua's feet were so large that one of his sandals could serve as bridge over the Rhône or Sarine, and his hands so strong that he tore great gaps in the Jura mountains to enable those two streams to make their way to the sea.

A mountain giant who roamed about in the mist, but never came down into the valleys, was known as Pathô. He delighted in terrifying the people in the lowlands by sudden wild cries, or by playfully rolling stones down upon them, their cattle, houses, or pastures.

Many of the Swiss giants were supposed to dwell in caves, or castles, on the tallest mountains, hidden from the eyes of men by ever-

shifting clouds. To commemorate this superstition, Chamisso wrote a charming ballad, telling
how the daughter of one of these giants once
strayed down into the valley, where, for the first
time in her life, she beheld a farmer ploughing
his field. In her delight and wonder, she bundled
man, horses, and plough into her apron, and
quickly carried them home, where she proudly
exhibited her new playthings to her father.
The giant, who wished the puny human race no
ill, immediately bade his little daughter carry the
frightened peasant and kicking team back to the
place where she had found them, gravely warning her never to meddle again with the people
in the valley, whose diligent toil supplied giants
as well as mortals with their daily bread.

THE monks who lived in the old abbey at
Romainmotier, in the northern part of the
canton of Vaud, once built a bridge over the
rushing waters of the Orbe, to enable the
throngs of pilgrims to reach a wonder-working
image of the Virgin near Vallorbes. But as
these monks were very eager to enrich their
monastery, they also placed a toll-gate across
the bridge, and would allow none to pass without paying a certain sum.

One night, the bridge-keeper was startled

out of his peaceful slumbers by the rhythmic sound of rapid hoof-beats on the hard road, and he sprang to his window just in time to find himself face to face with a panting, foam-flecked steed, upon which sat a girl clad in garments apparently no whiter than her anguished face. In breathless tones the maiden bade the keeper open wide the gate and let her pass, for her beloved mother was dangerously ill, and she wanted to plead for her recovery at the foot of the miraculous image.

The gate-keeper listened unmoved to this passionate entreaty, and instead of opening the gate, held it shut tight while sternly demanding his toll. In vain the girl repeated she had forgotten to bring any money, and implored him to let her pass, promising to bring him the required amount on the morrow ; he would not listen to anything she said.

Seeing it was useless to parley any longer with such an unfeeling man, yet determined to save her mother at any price, the brave girl urged her steed to the very edge of the bridge, and suddenly leaped over the low parapet into the rushing tide. For a few moments the horrified gate-keeper saw horse and rider struggling bravely to reach the opposite shore, but all at once their strength gave way, and they were swept into a whirlpool in the middle of the stream. A moment later he saw them dashed against sharp rocks, and vanish beneath the foaming waters which were soon tinged red with blood.

The gate-keeper stole back to his couch, trembling in every limb, but told no one of the girl's visit or of her frightful death. At midnight on the anniversary of the tragedy, the conscience-stricken man was however again roused by a loud clatter of hoofs. Torn from his bed by invisible hands, he found himself on the bridge, face to face with the same unhappy maid, whose snowy garments were now all stained with blood. Still impelled by a force he could not resist, the gate-keeper suddenly dropped down on his hands and knees before her, and felt her spring lightly upon his back. A second later he was galloping wildly toward the shrine of the miraculous Virgin.

There the maiden dismounted and fervently prayed for her sick mother ; then rising hastily from her knees, she again sprang upon her human steed, whom she urged on over the stony road by lashing him with a long wet reed. At the bridge, the spectre maiden vanished over the parapet, and the terrified gate-keeper straightened up once more, only in time to hear the gurgling cry of a drowning person rising above the roaring and splashing of the swollen stream.

This spectral apparition visited this man every year, and so shattered his nerves that he fell ill and died of fright. But before he breathed his last, he humbly confessed to one of the monks his cruel treatment of the girl, her pitiful end, and his awful punishment.

In memory of this event, an image of a man on all fours, and ridden by a beautiful maiden, was placed in the convent church, where it was long exhibited to pilgrims and tourists, to whom the above story is invariably told.

SOUTH of Romainmotier, on the road from Vallorbes to Lausanne, stands the small and very ancient town of La Sarraz, with its quaint castle. We are told that a statue was excavated there lately, which once stood in the chapel, and represented a knight, on whose cheeks and shoulder-blades clung loathsome toads. The recovery of that peculiar statue recalled the olden tale of a young knight of La Sarraz, who, having won great distinction in warfare, aspired to the hand of a Count's daughter.

Although the maiden was far above him in station, her father consented to their union, provided the bridegroom gave her a castle and three hundred cows as wedding gift, or *morgengabe*. This condition filled the knight's heart with hopeless sorrow, for he could boast no property except his trusty sword, his stout suit of mail, and his fiery battle-horse.

His parents, perceiving his dejection, questioned him tenderly, and when they learned the cause of his sorrow, they joyfully exclaimed that he need not despair, for they would give him castle and cattle, which was all they had in the world. They confidently added that they knew their son would never let them want in their old age, even if they did bestow everything upon him, reserving naught for themselves.

The selfish son gladly accepted this proffered sacrifice, but when the marriage ceremony had been completed, and he and his wife were comfortably settled in their . new home, he begrudged his old parents the little they required, and instigated by his wife, turned them out of the house one cold and stormy night.

After closing the door upon them, to shut off the sound of their pitiful sobs and heartbreaking reproaches, the knight of La Sarraz strode back into the hall of his castle, where a huge beaker of strong beer and a fine game-pie were awaiting him near a good fire. Settling himself down comfortably in a big armchair, the knight removed the crusty cover of the pie. But no sooner had he done so than he started back in horror, for two live toads sprang straight out of it to his cheeks, where they buried their claws so deep that no one could remove them. Every effort was made to kill these animals or drive them away, but all in vain. The knight, in despair, finally sent for the neighbouring priest, thinking that his prayers might accomplish what force and skill had failed to effect.

No sooner did the priest behold the live toads imbedded in the knight's cheeks, however, than he exclaimed this must be a visitation from heaven, and bade him confess what grievous sin he had committed. But when the knight acknowledged that he had unmercifully driven his aged parents out of the house they had given him, the priest made a frightened sign of the cross, and bade him apply to the bishop, as he could not give absolution for so heinous a sin.

The bishop, equally shocked and horrified at the knight's confession, referred him to the Pope, who, seeing the man's plight, bade him return to his native land, find his aged parents, atone for his past cruelty by treating them kindly as long as they lived, and assured him that when he had obtained their forgiveness, the toads would certainly depart from his face.

The knight of La Sarraz therefore journeyed home again, and after a long and conscientious search discovered the dead bodies of his old father and mother lying side by side in an abandoned hermitage. At the pitiful sight of their wasted corpses, he fell on his knees, while tears of bitter repentance flowed in torrents down his cheeks. These tears effected what no other agent had been able to accomplish, for the toads suddenly loosened their hold, and sprang from the knight's cheeks, down to his shoulders, where they again burrowed and clung fast.

As long as the knight of La Sarraz lived, he bore these awful living reminders of his sin, but as he kept them carefully hidden from sight, no one suspected the tortures he endured for more than twenty years. It is this sin and its awful punishment which was commemorated by the odd statue in the chapel of La Sarraz.

In the tenth century, when all the western part of Switzerland formed part of the kingdom of Burgundy, good Queen Bertha rode through the land, visiting every castle, farm, and hamlet,

and taking a kindly interest in the affairs of rich
and poor.

Wherever she went, she encouraged high and
low to be good and virtuous, setting them a
shining example of industry by spinning diligently from morning until night. Such was her
skill in handling the distaff, that she twirled it
even while riding her snow-white palfrey from
place to place. Those days were so peaceful
and happy, that the time " when Queen Bertha
span," is still regarded in Switzerland as a
synonym for the Golden Age. Of course, the
memory of so virtuous a ruler has been kept
green in the minds of the people, who have also
carefully preserved her saddle with its hole for
her distaff. This relic can still be seen in
Payerne, where the virtuous Queen lies buried
beside her husband and son.

Statues, pictures, and poems perpetuate Queen
Bertha's fame, and people still relate anecdotes
about her. One of these affirms that the queen,
seeing a shepherd girl spin while tending her
flock, was so delighted with her industry that
she bestowed upon her a rich reward. The
court ladies, wishing to secure similar benefits,
presented themselves on the morrow, distaff in
hand, before their royal mistress. Observing
them for a moment in silence, the queen then

archly remarked : " Ah, ladies ! the peasant girl, like Jacob, received the blessing because she came first, but you, like Esau, have come too late ! "

Queen Bertha was so good and charitable, that she was particularly loved by the poor, who claim that her spirit still haunts that region. Every year, towards Christmas time, she is said to wander through the villages after nightfall, peering in at every window to ascertain whether the women and girls have spun all their flax. Those who have been careful and diligent, and can show empty distaffs and skeins of fine, smooth thread, are rewarded by magic gifts. These consist of skeins which never end, or handfuls of leaves, twigs, shavings, or coal, which, if carefully put away, turn into gold before morning. But the maidens who have been careless or lazy are sure to be punished by sleepless nights, troubled dreams, tangled skeins, and numerous other petty mishaps.

We are told that Queen Bertha built the castle of Vufflens for a faithful servant who had become insane. As it was not safe to let him go abroad, the good Queen carefully selected this lovely spot so that the poor man could constantly feast his eyes upon the magnificent view of the lake, with Mont Blanc in the distance.

It is said that a thunderbolt put a sudden and merciful end to this madman's life. Then, as Queen Bertha was about to leave the country to join her married daughter in Lombardy, she bestowed the castle upon Grimoald, a brother of the deceased, believing him to be good and honourable too, although he was really a base-hearted wretch whom every one feared.

Grimoald had not deemed it necessary to marry until then, but, wishing to have an heir for his new castle, he soon brought home a reluctant bride, forced by a stern father to accept his hand. He treated his wife, Ermance, moderately well until the birth of her first child. But when he heard that this babe was a girl, instead of the boy he desired, he flew into a towering rage, and vowed it should be confined in one of the corner turrets of the castle, to remain there with its nurse until he had an heir. Poor Ermance pleaded in vain for an occasional glimpse, or even for news, of her child. Then, she began a series of pilgrimages, and fasted and prayed without ceasing, hoping that Providence would give her a son. To her intense sorrow, however, she gave birth to daughters only, who as soon as they came into the world were consigned to separate towers, their cruel father reiterating ever more emphatically the remarks he had made at the advent of his first child.

When the fourth daughter came, the poor mother, clasping her passionately in her arms, begged permission to share her imprisonment and be her nurse. Grimoald, whose wrath by this time knew no bounds, then angrily said :

" Since you can give me nothing but daughters, you may go ! But remember, I shall keep you in prison for ever. Every one shall believe you are dead, and I will take another wife, who, I hope, will not be such a fool as you ! "

Striding out of his wife's room, Grimoald then made all his arrangements. By his orders, the babe was carried to the turret, and Ermance covered with a sheet as if she were dead. Then a coffin was brought into the room by servants, who fancied their mistress had died of grief at losing her fourth child too. But during the night, Raymond, Grimoald's trusted henchman, put some stones into this coffin, nailed down the lid, and secretly conveyed his mistress to the fourth tower, which, like all the rest, then communicated with his own dwelling by secret passageways.

Years now passed by, during which Ermance devoted all her thoughts to her last child, for her husband had made Raymond tell her that

the other little girls were all dead.   From a
narrow window high up in the wall, she caught
a glimpse of her funeral procession ; but although
she often saw her husband ride in and out of
the castle yard, she never beheld a woman
beside him, for now that his cruelty was known,
no one would consent to marry him.

Although confined within the narrow limits
of a little tower room, Ermance's youngest
daughter throve like a flower, and became so
pretty and attractive that she won the heart
of her grim jailer. Before she was thirteen,
Raymond could refuse her nothing, and when
he fell ill, he sent his adopted son and daughter
to wait upon her and her mother. In the company of these charming young people, — to
whom mother and daughter felt equally attracted,
— the prisoners spent many happy hours, and
heard many tidings of the outside world.

In the meantime Grimoald was failing fast,
and Raymond rushed into the tower one night
to summon his mistress and her daughter to his
master's death-bed. On entering her husband's
chamber, Ermance was somewhat surprised to
behold there Raymond's adopted children with
two other beautiful girls. But she almost died
of joy, when Grimoald faintly informed her
that these three maidens were the children for

whom she had mourned so long. Then, after begging and obtaining her forgiveness for all he had made her endure, Grimoald told her that Raymond's adopted son, the child of an elder brother, was to inherit the castle of Vufflens, where, however, she and her daughters might dwell as long as they pleased.

Neither Ermance nor her daughters could mourn greatly for a husband and father who had treated them so cruelly, and after he was laid to rest, they openly rejoiced to find themselves free to go wherever they pleased. The four girls, especially, were in a state of rapturous delight over everything they heard and saw ; for, until then, their world had consisted of narrow turret chambers, with as much of the country as they could perceive from loop-hole windows.

In time, three of these maidens, who were noted for their great beauty, married the lords of Blonay, Châtelard, and La Sarraz, whose castles still exist to-day, while the fourth became the wife of Artus, the new and gallant young lord of Vufflens. Unlike his uncle, this knight treated his wife and children with the utmost consideration, and the corner turrets were never again used as prisons for innocent babes.

In journeying on eastward along the northern shore of the Lake of Geneva, one soon comes to a dense forest of pine and hickory, very near Clarens, where stands the famous overhanging "Scex que Plliau," or Raining Rock, of which the following romantic legend is told :

The son of a rich lord, whose castle was at Montreux, once fell desperately in love with Joliette, the daughter of a neighbouring mountaineer. All went well until the young man's father heard of this love affair. and peremptorily bade his son part for ever from the maiden who was too far beneath him in station ever to become his wife.

The young lover, unwilling to give up his beloved, yet not daring to see her openly, now began to roam about the country, ostensibly in quest of game, but in reality in hope of encountering by chance the fair Joliette. One day, the good fairies who watch over all true lovers of that region, brought both young people to a charming and secluded spot in the forest, and while they sat there under an overhanging rock, exchanging vows and confidences, the hours sped by unmarked.

They were still lingering there, hand in hand, listening to the soughing of the wind in the pines, and the ripple of the waters over the stony bed of

Clarens Bay, when they were suddenly startled out of their love dream by the angry voice of the young man's father. Terrified beyond measure by this unwelcome interruption, Joliette fled for protection to the arms of her lover, who, clasping her close to his heart, gazed defiantly at his sire.

The baron of Chaulin, however, like all mediæval fathers, expected his son to obey him implicitly ; so when he beheld this attitude, he angrily bade his followers hurl the disobedient lovers over the rocks into the ravine at their feet ! But, before this fierce order could be carried out, Albert sprang in front of Joliette with drawn sword, swearing he would have the life blood of any one who dared to lay a finger upon his betrothed.

His resolute bearing checked for a moment the advance of the baron's followers, who had tried to execute their master's order. While they stood there motionless, silently awaiting further directions, a fairy voice was suddenly heard, bidding the young people marry without fear, promising them her protection, and upbraiding the hard-hearted father for opposing their union. This speech, which somewhat encouraged the lovers, further exasperated the baron. He furiously bade his men seek for the witch and hang her on the nearest tree, adding that his son should marry Joliette when water dripped through the rock above them, but not before !

To emphasise this statement, the baron savagely kicked the stone with his mailed heel, and he was about to pour forth more abuse, when he suddenly beheld the rock turn damp and saw the first drop of water form and fall. All now gazed in open-mouthed wonder at the overhanging rock, to which clung countless big drops which fell one after another, with a gentle splash, while new ones formed above in their stead.

" The rock is raining, the rock is raining ! " the baron's followers gasped ; and then, seized with superstitious terror, they turned and fled, leaving their master alone with the lovers.

" Yes," cried the fairy's voice, " the rock is raining, and unless the baron of Chaulin breaks his word for the first time in his life, you young people can now marry without further delay."

Awed by this phenomenon, or too honourable to disregard his oath, the baron not only consented to the young people's union, but gave them such a grand wedding that all Montreux feasted and danced for a whole week.

Since then, water has constantly trickled from

the overhanging Raining Rock, down on the moss and the shiny-leaved water plants beneath it ; and the delicate fronds of the ferns, growing in every cranny, perpetually rise and fall with dainty grace as the huge drops fall down upon them, and glancing off, slowly roll from stone to stone until they find their way into the Lake of Geneva.

NORTH of Clarens, on the boundary of the cantons of Vaud and Fribourg, is the mighty Dent de Jaman, which can best be crossed by means of the "col," or pass. of the same name.

A peasant who had never left his native valley in the southern part of the canton of Fribourg, once decided that it might be well to see a little of the world, and after talking a long while of his plans, he bade his friends and relatives an impressive farewell and set out. Armed with his mountain staff, he slowly climbed the rough path leading to the Col de Jaman. Tramping sturdily on, he soon came to the boundary line between his own canton and that of Vaud. Never yet had he ventured so far from home, and everything seemed so strange that he kept looking around and behind him, marvelling at the view, which grew more and more extended with every step.

As it was one of those bright days when every object is perceptible for miles around, there was plenty to see, and as he had never travelled, he was quite unprepared for the sight which greeted his eyes when he reached the top of the pass. He therefore stood still there, in open-mouthed wonder, his gaze fixed upon the wonderful Lake of Geneva, whose waters were of the exact tint of the sky overhead.

After staring thus for some time, the sturdy peasant heaved a great sigh, turned slowly on his hobnailed heel, and wended his way home again, along the very path which he had just trod.

When he reached his native village once more, the people all crowded around him, asking why he had come back so soon, and what had induced him to give up his long-cherished plan to see the world on the other side of the mountain?

The peasant, whose intellect was none of the keenest, listened stolidly to all their questions, then, scratching his curly head, slowly explained that on reaching the top of the pass he had discovered it would be useless and rather unsafe to venture any farther, as a big piece of the sky had just dropped down into the valley on the other side of the mountain!

A SIMPLE mountaineer, whose greatest ambition was to own a horse, worked and saved with the utmost diligence until he had amassed a sum sufficient to purchase a colt. Thinking it would be very delightful to watch the gradual development of this animal into the coveted steed, the good man tied up his savings in a corner of his handkerchief, and taking his sharpest-pointed staff set out long before day-break for Aigle, where he knew a large horse and cattle fair was held.

After a long, fatiguing tramp down the steep Ormond mountains, the sturdy mountaineer reached the valley, and entering the town of Aigle, proceeded to examine every horse and foal on the market, with the laudable aim of securing the best animal he could for his money. Pricing them one after another, he found, to his intense dismay, that his savings were not sufficient to pay for the smallest colt offered for sale there, and that he would have to return home without having made the desired purchase.

A charlatan, who had slyly watched him for some time, now stepped up to him, and before long drew from the unsophisticated mountaineer a detailed account of his long cherished hopes and of his present bitter disappointment.

3

After listening with feigned sympathy to the whole story, the charlatan suggested that if the peasant's means would not permit his buying a foal, he ought to purchase a mare's egg; adding that a cow could hatch it, and suckle the foal until it was old enough to eat grass.

The peasant, delighted with this suggestion, promptly expressed a fervent desire to buy a mare's egg if such a treasure could only be secured. Assuring him there would be no difficulty about that, the charlatan led the peasant to another part of the town, and after threading his way amid countless bags and baskets of fruit and vegetables exposed for sale, he finally stopped before a cart in which lay a huge yellow squash.

"There is a fine mare's egg!" cried the charlatan to the peasant, making a sign to his accomplice, the proprietor of both squash and cart. The mountaineer, who had never seen a squash in his life, stared at it in awe and wonder, and after asking countless questions and doing considerable chaffering, he decided to purchase it. To carry it home safely, he then tied it up in his huge handkerchief, which he hung on the end of his stick over his shoulder.

He was so elated by his purchase, and by the potations he had indulged in with his friend, the charlatan, while closing the bargain, that he set out for home trolling a merry song. Climbing higher and higher, he revelled in joyful anticipations of his wife's surprise, and of the time when the huge egg he carried would be safely hatched and a pretty foal would come at his call.

While walking near the edge of a precipice, glancing from time to time down its steep sides covered with jagged rocks and stunted bushes, the knots in the handkerchief, loosened by the weight of the squash, suddenly came undone, and the startled peasant beheld his precious purchase bounding from rock to rock down the precipitous slope! As he stood there, motionless in utter despair, the squash dashed with such force against a sharp stone that it flew into pieces which scattered far and wide.

At the same moment, a brown hare, hiding in a bush near by, sprang in terror from its cover and darted down the mountain. The peasant, thinking this was the desired colt, accidentally released from the shattered egg, loudly called: "Coltie, Coltie, come here!" and wrung his hands in helpless grief when he saw the fleet brown creature disappear.

After vainly watching for hours for its return, the peasant sorrowfully went home, and spent the evening relating his various adventures to his wife. And, as long as he lived, he talked of the remarkable horse which he would have had, had not the fleet-footed colt run away as soon as hatched from the mare's egg bought on the market-place at Aigle.

THE mountains around Ormont were once remarkably rich in game of all kinds, and the favourite haunts of large herds of chamois. Tradition claims that these animals were herded on the high pastures by countless dwarfs, the servants of the august Spirit of the Alps. Chamois-hunters who slew too many of these deer, or who ventured high up the mountains and along the dizzy precipices where they were supposed to be safe from human reach, were sure to be punished for their temerity. Either the Spirit of the Alps appeared to them in person (as in Schiller's poem of the Chamois Hunter), bidding them begone in awe-inspiring tones, or dwarfs uttered similar warnings. When some rash mortal ventured to disobey these orders, the gnomes slyly laid bits of treacherous ice under his feet, or deftly loosed the rocks on which he trod, thus making him lose his precarious foothold and fall into some abyss, where he was dashed to pieces.

The chamois-hunters of the region not only delighted in this venturesome sport, but prided themselves upon constantly adding new victims to their hunting record, which was always kept with scrupulous care. Some of these men, wandering up to almost inaccessible heights, are said to have encountered there dainty, mist-like Alpine fairies, who guided them safely over dangerous places, watched over their slumbers when they rested exhausted at the edge of frightful precipices, and often whispered wonderful dream tales into their drowsy ears.

Both dwarfs and fairies are also reported to have revealed to their favourites the places where the finest rock crystals could be found, to have delivered into their keeping long-concealed treasures, or to have bestowed upon them magic bullets which never missed their aim, or cheeses made of chamois milk, which became whole again after every meal, provided a small piece was left " for manners."

As the chamois are the shyest of game, and their brown coats are not easily distinguishable at a distance from the rocks, hunters often carry spy-glasses to locate their quarry. We are told that one of these men, discovering that the chamois were sure to see him and scamper away before he could lay down his glass and take good aim, once decided that it would be of great assistance to him if he could only see and shoot around the corner of any rock behind which he chose to hide. After much cogitation, therefore, this particular hunter bent his gun and spy-glass so they formed sharp angles. Thanks to this clever device, he easily discovered and killed his prey!

Another sportsman once set out with his pack of dogs to hunt hares. He had not gone very far before seven fine specimens, starting from covert, darted away. The hounds eagerly pursued six of them, but the hunter concentrated all his attention upon the seventh and last, which was also the finest. This hare, however, was as sly as it was large and fleet-footed, and knowing the man's unerring aim, began to run around and around a haycock. Such was the speed with which the hare ran, that the hunter's eyes could not follow it, and even the animal's shadow failed to keep up with it. The sportsman, seeing he would never bag this fine hare unless he too resorted to stratagem, quickly bent the barrel of his gun until it almost formed a hoop. Then, taking quick aim, he sent after the speeding hare a bullet which laid it low in its circular track around the haycock.

ALPINE FAY.

In olden times Wotan reigned alone in the canton of Vaud, to which he is said to have given his local name Vaudai. As long as he was sole master of the country, Wotan proved on the whole an amiable and benevolent ruler; but the gradual introduction of Christianity so soured his temper and made him behave so badly, that the Christians finally identified him with the Evil One himself.

The new religion was so very distasteful to Wotan, that he hated both sight and sound of it, and hoping to avoid coming in contact with it, retreated far up into the mountains and took up his abode on the summit of the Diablerets. There, he vented his rage by sending dense fogs and violent storms down into the valleys, and by producing great snow-storms so that the melting drifts should cause all the rivers to overflow.

Brooding over his wrongs one day, Wotan determined to make a last and mighty effort to exterminate Christianity in the Rhône valley by drowning all the inhabitants. He therefore called up a fearful storm, and at his command the river began to boil and rise and overflow. Riding on the crest of a huge wave, Wotan himself swept down the valley, while the waters rose higher and higher, threatening to wash away everything along their path. But all

Wotan's magic proved powerless when he came in sight of St. Maurice, where the Christians had set up a huge cross. Before this holy emblem the waters suddenly cowed, crept back into their wonted place, and flowed peacefully on within their long-appointed limits.

Baffled and discouraged, Wotan again re-treated to the Diablerets, where he is said to beguile the monotony of his sojourn by holding monster witch-dances on certain nights of the year. All the spirits, witches, and sorcerers of the neighbourhood then betake themselves on their broomstick-steeds to the Diablerets, to indulge in mad revelry. They circle around so wildly in their sabbatical dances that the motion raises a wind which sweeps down the mountain on all sides, while the sounds of their cries, hisses, and flying footsteps can often be heard far down the valley.

THE souls of all those who have done wrong while on earth are also supposed to haunt the top-most ridges of the Diablerets, where they play endless games of ninepins with the demons and their master. This belief is so general that in speaking of a dead sinner the natives gen-erally say, "Oh, he has gone to join the demons on the Diablerets!" instead of stating that he has gone to Hades to receive due punishment for his crimes. Besides, one of the peaks of that mountain is called the Devil's Ninepin ; and when a great clatter is heard on the glacier, the people whisper in awestruck tones that the spirits are evidently engaged in their infernal game. When stones come clattering down on the pastures, the shepherds think they are some of the spirits' missiles which have strayed out of bounds, and they seek to ward off the nearer approach of evil by repeated and fervent signs of the cross.

On the way to Chamounix, far above the road, you can perceive the entrance of the famous stalactite Grotte de Balme, the supposed abode of all the fairies of that region. These creatures resembled human maidens, except that they were dark of skin and had no heels to their feet. Clad in long rippling hair, which fell all around them like a garment, the fairies of Balme often sought to lure young shepherds and hunters into their retreat. Sometimes, too, they met these men on lonely mountain paths, where they tried to win their affections by gifts of rare Alpine flowers, of fine rock crystals, of lumps of gold and silver, or by teaching them the use of the healing herbs and showing them how to discover hidden treasures. The youths who refused the fairies' advances encountered such resentment that they were sure to meet shortly afterwards with some fatal accident. Those who ventured on the Diablerets, or the Oldenhorn, for instance, were suddenly pushed over the rocks into abysses and crevasses, from whence they never escaped alive.

But the young men who received the fairies' overtures graciously were very well treated, and a few of them were even taken up to the grotto, where they feasted on choice game, and quaffed fiery wine as long as they obeyed their fairy wives. If, however, they proved untrustworthy, or tried to pry into the fairies' secrets, they were ignominiously dismissed; and while some of them managed to return home, the majority never prospered again, and as a rule came to an untimely end.

BEFORE the Rhône enters the Lake of Geneva, and not very far from Noville, there are low banks and a few picturesque little islands, all covered with lush grass, and bordered with rustling reeds and shiny-leaved water-plants of all kinds.

These marshy places, with their dense luxuriant vegetation, are said to be the favourite haunts of fairies and nixies of all kinds, and especially of a local water-nymph known as Fenetta. All the river sprites timidly avoid the glance of man ; so it is only now and then that some sharp-eyed native catches the gleam of a white hand gently parting the tall reeds, or discerns a slender figure, garbed in trailing white robes all dripping with water, and wearing a wreath of water-lilies upon her rippling golden hair.

The water-nymphs betray their presence only by a slight rustle among the reeds, by an almost inaudible whisper, or by a long-drawn trembling sigh. But at dawn and twilight their breath is so cold and clammy, that whenever it happens to strike a mortal, cold shivers begin to creep up and down his spine, his finger-nails turn blue, and before long his teeth chatter noisily. Then, if the victim looks behind him, he is pretty sure to descry somewhere among the reeds on the bank a mist-like trail, which is the flutter of the water-nymph's white veil.

Although the river-sprites are lovely in appearance, none of the people care to see them, for those whose eyes have rested upon them have invariably died within a year. For that reason, the banks of the stream are generally deserted after sunset. the hour when the fairies

are wont to sally forth to disport themselves
in the cool waters of the limpid river, to tread
the measures of their noiseless but fantastic
dances along the shore, or to flit from one
water-lily to another, gently opening their waxen
petals with cool and dainty fingers.

Even in broad daylight it is well to shun
these marshy places, and those who do venture
there should always warn the nymphs of their
approach by whistling, singing, or making some
other marked sound. Such signals enable the
fairies to scurry out of sight before the visitor
draws near ; and when he reaches the bank,
waving reeds and grasses are the only sign of
an unseen presence.

It is said that a coquettish maiden from
Noville once bade her lover go and get
her some water-lilies, although she knew the
hour had struck when the water-sprites had
left their retreat. The young man, who had
frequently declared he did not believe there
were any water-nymphs, cheerfully departed to
do her bidding. Running down to the river's
edge, he hastily unfastened his skiff, and with
long and vigorous strokes rowed out to the
place where the water-lilies softly rose and
fell on the rippling waters in the midst of their
broad green leaves.

THE MIST NYMPH.

The last golden gleams had just died out in the west, gray shadows had replaced the flush on the snow mountains, and a cool evening breeze was sweeping gently over the river. The young man, who had laboured under the burning sun all day, revelled in the freshness all around him, and although he caught glimpses of vapoury white here and there along the shore, he thought they were trails of mist, and smiled to himself because superstitious mortals mistook them for the flutter of the nymphs' gossamer veils.

He was just bending over the edge of the boat to reach the largest and finest lily, when he felt an icy breath on his neck, and turning around with a start, dimly perceived Fenetta's lovely form, and noticed that she was sadly and gently motioning to him to depart. As she vanished, he suddenly felt cold chills running all over him, and looking downward perceived that his sunburned hands seemed strangely wan and pale. With chattering teeth and failing strength he now rowed back to the shore ; but although he grew colder and colder every minute, and felt as if the chill had gone to his very heart, he picked up the lilies to carry them to his beloved.

Reaching her door with faltering steps, he swooned on the threshold, scattering the lilies at the feet of the maiden, who came out to welcome him with merry words and arch smiles. At first she fancied he had merely tripped, but seeing he did not immediately rise, she stooped over him barely in time to catch his last sigh and a faint whisper of " Fenetta! Fenetta!"

The sudden death of this stalwart young lover proved such a shock to the maiden of Noville, that she lost her reason and began to wander along the river-bank among the reeds, constantly murmuring "Fenetta! Fenetta!"

The nymph, in pity for her sorrow, must have appeared to her too; for one evening she came home with dripping garments and shivering from head to foot. After a few days' illness, the girl gently passed away, still whispering the water-nymph's name; and since then youths and maidens have carefully avoided this fatal spot after sundown.

In the valley of Conthey, noted for its picturesque situation as well as for its wines, there once dwelt a tailor who made fun of his wife because she firmly believed in witches, ghosts, and spirits of all kinds, and even maintained that a helpful sprite assisted her when she had more work on hand than she could easily accomplish.

The tailor, who had been freely tasting the vintage of some of his neighbours, once mockingly remarked, while sitting cross-legged upon his bench, that he wished her familiar spirit would appear and take him on a nightly journey through the Valais, for he would like to see the famous witches and demons about which he had heard so many tales.

The words were scarcely out of his mouth, when a grinning, mischievous dwarf, clad in all the colours of the rainbow, suddenly darted out of a corner, saying, " Your wish shall be granted ! " At the same moment the tailor felt a clawlike hand close over his coat-collar, and was whisked through the air to Monthey. There, he and the dwarf alighted on the banks of the Viege, while the clocks were solemnly tolling the midnight hour, and quickly mounted a coal-black ram which came rushing out of the churchyard to meet them. The dwarf, who had jerked the tailor on the ram's back, roughly bade him hold fast, whispering that their fleet-footed steed was the spectral ram of Monthey, which ranged noisily through the land on certain days in the year.

They now sped on so fast that the tailor felt the wind whistle through his hair, and he almost fainted with terror when his guide pointed

out the huge Ivy Snake, which was mounting
guard over all the gold of heathendom, spread
out on a barren heath. The snake no sooner
perceived them than it rushed towards them,
hissing loudly and breathing fire and brimstone
from its gaping mouth. A timely kick, admin-
istered by the dwarf, fortunately urged the
black ram on to such speed, that the Ivy
Snake could not overtake them however fast
it pursued.

At St. Maurice the ram paused for a moment
near the monastery fish-pond, where a dead
trout suddenly rose to the surface of the
water.

" There," cried the dwarf, " one of the
choristers has just died, for whenever one of
them breathes his last, a dead trout appears in
this pond."

In confirmation of his words, a funeral knell
began to toll, and this sound accompanied them
for some time as they sped on towards the
Plan Nevé. Here, among the gray rocks and
along the huge glacial stream, they beheld
countless barefooted ghosts painfully threading
their way. The dwarf then explained to the
tailor that these spirits were condemned to
carry fine sand up the mountain in sieves, but
that as every grain ran out long before they

reached their goal, they were obliged to begin again and again their hopeless task.

At the bottom of a neighbouring well, the dwarf next pointed out the ghost of Nero, who, in punishment for his manifold sins, was condemned to blow huge bubbles up to the surface without ever stopping to rest. In the Aucenda, near Gex, the dwarf also showed him the spirits of dishonest lawyers, who, having fished in figuratively troubled waters all their lives, were now condemned to do the same in the ice-cold stream, where they were further employed in brewing the storms and freshets which desolate that region.

Before the bewildered tailor had time to comment upon these awful sights, he was whisked away to La Soye, where a red-headed maiden told him she would give him a golden calf, provided he would kiss her thrice. Reasoning that it was far from Conthey, and that his wife could not possibly see him. the tailor pursed up his lips, and was about to bestow the first kiss, when the red-headed girl was suddenly transformed into a hideous, writhing dragon. This metamorphosis so terrified the poor tailor that he buried his heels in the flanks of the black ram, which darted away at such a rattling pace that they soon reached Sion.

There the dwarf transferred the tailor to the back of the three-legged white horse which haunts this city, and as they galloped away, the tailor saw that they were followed by a fire-breathing boar, the ram, the dragon, the red-headed girl, the ghosts of Plan Nevé with their sieves, and the dripping lawyers. In the dim distance he could also descry Nero, still blowing huge bubbles, and the deceased chorister holding a dead trout between his teeth.

This strange procession now swept along the Rhône valley to the Baths of Leuk, where they were joined by a mischievous sprite who rapped loudly at every door as he darted past. At Zauchet, their ranks were further increased by the wraith of a giant ox, whose horns glowed like live coals and whose tail consisted of a flaming torch.

Next they sped down the Visp valley, where a woman once refused food to Our Lord when he journeyed through the land. In punishment for this sin, the hamlet where she dwelt sank beneath the ground, and a stream now runs over the broad, flat stone which formed the altar of the village church.

Arriving at Zermatt, the dwarf and tailor exchanged their mount for a blue-haired donkey, whose loud bray, added to the snorts, groans, hisses, and cries of their ghostly train, created an awful din in the peaceful valleys through which they swept like the wind. Arriving finally at Lake Champey, the Blue Ass swam to an island, where the Devil of Corbassière and a number of witches were madly treading the swift measures of an infernal dance.

The tailor, seeing this, sprang from his steed to join them; but when he offered to kiss the youngest and prettiest of the witches, the Devil of Corbassière angrily flung him head first into the lake. As the witches belaboured him with their broomsticks whenever he tried to creep ashore on the island, the tailor finally struck out for the other bank, where he sank down, panting and exhausted, and closed his eyes.

Suddenly he felt a small hand laid upon him, and thinking it must be one of his recent tormentors, he cried aloud in terror, "Leave me alone, you witch!"

A vigorous box on his ear made him open his eyes with a start, just in time to see his wife standing over him with upraised hand, saying, "I'll teach you to call me a witch!"

The tailor now protested that he had done nothing of the kind; but although his wife declared that he had merely fallen asleep over his work, he knew that his spirit had journeyed all

through the Valais, in company with the dwarf
and the demons which haunt the land.

He was so thoroughly imbued with this belief
that he never made fun of his wife's supersti-
tions again, and when sceptics denied the existence of ghosts, demons, or witches, he merely
shook his head, for he had seen for himself that
" there are more things in heaven and earth
than are dreamt of in our philosophy."

THE ascension of the Fletschhorn, near the
Simplon, was probably first accomplished in
1856, but tradition claims that this feat was
performed long before this date by a dauntless
Swiss.

He resolved to be the first to reach the top
of the mountain, and with that object in view
started to scale it early one fine morning. As
he did not know which road to follow, he
scrambled up and down the rocks, through
snow and over ice, and thus was quite exhausted long before he came near the top,
where jagged rocks and steep walls of ice
offer only a most precarious foothold.

The mountaineer, who was an expert climber,
knew it would be folly to venture any farther
that day, so he sat down to rest a moment before he began the descent. While sitting there

on the mountain side, trying to recover his breath, he suddenly heard a ghostly voice far above him, bidding him bring a cat, dog, and cock, as propitiatory sacrifices to the Spirit of the Mountain next time he attempted the ascent.

Refreshed by a few days' rest and by strengthening food, the mountaineer soon set out again, taking with him the three animals the Mountain Spirit had asked for. At the first dangerous spot the dog lost his foothold and fell down a precipice; farther on even the cat's sharp claws failed to preserve it from slipping down into the blue-green depths of a crevasse, and after some more rough climbing the cold grew so intense that the poor cock was frozen stiff!

The brave mountaineer now pressed on alone, although it was snowing hard and the wind blew sharp ice splinters into his face which almost blinded him. Presently the storm began to rage with such fury that the man had to relinquish his purpose, although he had now reached a much higher point than the first time.

On arriving home, friends and neighbours crowded around him, to hear a minute account of his adventures; but they all deemed him more than foolhardy when he declared that, in spite of

all the perils encountered, he meant to try again
on the next favourable day.

True to his resolve, however, the man started
out again with cat, dog, and cock, which poor
animals met with the same fate as their pre-
decessors. As for the Swiss himself, he climbed
higher and higher, until he came so near the
summit that a last determined effort would have
enabled him to reach it. But the great exertions he had made, and the rarefied atmosphere,
brought on a severe headache which made him
feel very weak and dizzy. Nevertheless he
bravely went on until the pain in his head grew
so intolerable that it seemed as if his skull
would burst. He therefore relinquished his
attempt, and crept slowly home, feeling his headache decrease with every downward step.

But even this last experience could not daunt
our climber, who set out again a few days later,
with the same strange trio of animals. This
time, however, he prudently provided himself
with an iron hoop, which fitting closely around
his head, would prevent its bursting should he
again reach a great altitude !

Thus equipped, he wended his way up the
Fletschhorn, where cat, dog, and rooster soon
perished, leaving the man to continue his perilous climb alone. Although the pain in his

head again grew worse with every upward step, our mountaineer pressed bravely on, knowing the iron band would hold fast, and finally reached the topmost pinnacle of the mountain. His fellow-citizens, proud of this feat, bestowed upon him the Fletschalp, and honoured him as long as he lived as the most skilful Alpine climber of that part of the country.

PATCHES of so-called red snow are sometimes found high up on the Alps ; but while scientists ascribe that peculiar colour to a microscopic fungus growth, the legend accounts for the vivid hue in a very different way.

In bygone times, before the Alps had been pierced by tunnels and even before convenient roadways had been built, rough paths leading over the various passes served as means of communication between Switzerland and Italy. These were much frequented by pack-drivers with their sure-footed mules, and among other things thus imported were fiery Italian wines. Some of the muleteers who had a tendency to drink, or who were none too scrupulous to cheat their employers, used to tap the barrels and kegs on their way over the mountains, replacing the wine they had consumed by water from some mountain stream, so that the vessels were always full when they reached their destination.

The pack-drivers on the Furka Pass were, it seems, especially addicted to this species of peculation, and generally paused at the top of the pass to refresh themselves after their long and arduous climb. In their eagerness to partake of the strength-giving fluid, some of them often tapped their barrels so hastily that red wine spurted forth, and falling upon the immaculate snow gave it a blood-like tinge.

In punishment for this crime, or for so carelessly guarding their merchandise that they did not even notice when barrels leaked, many pack-drivers are now said to haunt this pass, continually treading the path they once went over. They are tormented by a thirst such as is known by the damned only, and which all the ice, snow, and running streams around there cannot quench. Their only refreshment now comes from the scattered drops remaining here and there upon the snow, or from small libations which compassionate travellers still pour out along the pass, to moisten the parched lips and throats of these unhappy spirits.

THE old and picturesque city of Grandson, on the west shore of Lake Neuchâtel, and in the northern part of the canton of Vaud, is noted in history as the place where, in 1476, fifty thousand Burgundians, under their Duke Charles the Bold, were routed with great slaughter by less than half that number of Swiss patriots. Rich and quaint specimens of the booty secured on that memorable occasion by the victors, still adorn various Swiss museums and arsenals; Soleure exhibiting the costume of Charles's jester, while Lucerne boasts of the golden Seal of Burgundy.

Many romantic legends are told of the town and castle of Grandson, which were defended by a Bernese patriot, Brandolf of Stein, at the beginning of the Burgundian war. Such was the courage and skill of this commander, that, perceiving he could not secure the town by force, the Count of Romont, Charles's ally, resorted to stratagem. It succeeded only too well, and the Burgundians were already masters of the town when the first alarm was given, and Stein rushed bravely into the fray at the head of his five hundred men. The Swiss, however, soon saw that the town was lost, and wishing to preserve the castle until his countrymen could send reinforcements to eject the Burgundians, Stein quickly ordered a retreat.

To make sure that the enemy would be held

at bay until all his men were safe, and the castle gates duly closed, Stein himself covered their retreat ; but at the last moment he was surrounded and overpowered by Romont, who, forcing him to surrender, led him away to his own quarters to await the arrival and decree of the Duke.

As soon as Charles came, he bade Romont lead Stein under the walls of the castle, and have a herald proclaim that unless the garrison surrendered immediately, Stein would be put to death. This order was executed ; but the last words of the proclamation had scarcely been uttered when the prisoner sternly cried, —

"Comrades, pay no heed to these summons. You were Swiss before you became my friends ; therefore be true to your country, and die rather than relinquish your trust. But if you love me, guard well my treasure and cast it into the lake rather than let it fall into the hands of our enemy."

Before the Burgundians could recover sufficient presence of mind to silence him, this brief speech was ended, and it was clear that not a word of it had been lost, for the garrison shouted a unanimous refusal to yield when summoned to do so for the third and last time. Still, when the Swiss saw their beloved chief led away to the scaffold, hot tears poured freely down their bronzed and bearded cheeks.

Such was their respect for their master's memory that they resisted every attack, holding out until forged papers convinced them that Bern was in the power of the Burgundians, and that they could expect no help from their distressed countrymen. These false tidings determined them to surrender the castle, provided their safety was guaranteed by Charles the Bold.

But the gates were no sooner opened than Charles, in spite of his promises, ordered most of these brave men cast into the lake or hanged, sparing only a few of those who pledged themselves to serve him faithfully. Having thus rid himself of the garrison, the Duke next proceeded to search for Stein's treasure, but all in vain. He questioned the few survivors, but they truthfully declared they had never heard of any store of gold, silver, or precious stones. Convinced nevertheless that Stein must have owned at least one priceless jewel, Charles bitterly regretted having slain him before ascertaining the nature and place of concealment of that treasure.

Thinking that Laurent, keeper of the alarm tower, an old retainer of Stein's, might know

something about it. Charles went in quest of
him, harshly threatening to pitch him into the
lake, unless he immediately revealed all he
knew concerning his master's possessions. Thus
constrained, Laurent reluctantly admitted that
Stein, having spared the life of a Mussulman,
had received from this grateful man a pyramidal
diamond of fabulous value, from which hung
by a slender golden chain a huge pear-shaped
pearl.

The Duke, who had a passion for diamonds,
immediately ordered a new and more minute
search ; but as the treasure was not forthcoming, he renewed his visit and threats, telling
Laurent he must produce the missing jewel or
die on the spot. In vain the poor man swore
he had never seen the diamond since his mistress wore it on her wedding-day ; the Duke
refused to believe him, and angrily ordered him
flung out of the window ! Just then, however,
a panel in the wall directly opposite Charles
slipped noiselessly aside, revealing a deep niche
in which stood a beautiful, stern-faced woman,
gowned all in black, but wearing a dazzling
diamond pendant. This woman stepped slowly
forward, the panel closed behind her, and the
Duke started back in terror when she threw
the magnificent jewel at his feet, crying, —

" There, traitor, behold the diamond you covet ; but Stein's real treasures, his sorrowing wife and innocent daughter, will die by their own hand rather than fall into the power of such a miscreant as you ! "

Then, before the Duke could recover sufficient presence of mind to speak or move, the Lady of Stein vanished behind the secret panel, and Charles could have believed himself victim of a delusion had not the jewel still sparkled at his feet.

The Lady of Stein had vanished ; but the Burgundian now learned from Laurent that the two ladies were waiting, in the secret chambers of the castle, for an opportunity to escape to a convent. where both intended to take the veil, since he had broken their hearts by killing Stein.

Charles, who had an eye for beauty, promptly reasoned that the daughter of such a handsome mother must be very lovely, and he began to devise an excuse to see her. He therefore artfully informed Laurent that Romont alone was to blame for Stein's death ; adding that his dearest wish was to provide a suitable husband for Elizabeth Stein, and that, in token of regard, he would give her her father's jewel as wedding present. Then he persuaded Laurent to carry

a message to his stern mistress and induce her
to come down into the great hall of the castle,
where he would await her.

The Duke having departed, Laurent touched
a cunningly hidden spring, and threaded his
way along secret passages which led from tower
to tower, down long, narrow stairs, and into a
passageway opening out on the lake. In one
of these recesses he found his mistress, who
finally consented to appear before Charles with
her seventeen-year-old daughter Elizabeth.

The moment Charles's eyes rested upon this
lovely maiden, he was seized with a mad passion, which he determined to gratify at any
cost. His first move was to try and gain the
good graces of both women, but in spite of all
his protestations and courteous speeches, the
Lady of Stein declared he must prove his innocence by punishing her husband's murderer,
adding that her daughter would either marry
her father's avenger or become a nun.

On hearing these words, Charles gave immediate orders to seize Romont and have him
beheaded in the presence of both ladies. A
few moments later, therefore, the Count stood
in the castle yard ; but when the executioner
read aloud his death sentence, he boldly declared he was neither a murderer nor a traitor,

and that he could prove his innocence, were the guest in his tent only allowed to appear with him before Charles. Anxious to seem just and generous in the eyes of the ladies, the Duke granted this request, and the brave young James of Romont soon came in, followed by a man in full armour.

" My lord Duke," cried Romont, "I am not a traitor! I have merely been guilty of disobeying an order which I knew you would regret in time. You accuse me of being Stein's murderer; that is impossible, for, behold! there he stands!"

At that moment the stranger to whom Romont pointed threw up his vizor, and both ladies rapturously flew into his arms, thus proving his unmistakable identity. The first outburst of emotion over, Stein told his wife and daughter how generously Romont had treated him, and Charles winced when he heard them express their undying gratitude, and saw the glances exchanged by the young people, who had fallen in love with each other at first sight.

To rid himself of the youthful saviour who found such evident favour in Elizabeth's eyes, Charles now sternly ordered Romont back to prison, saying he must prove himself innocent of the charge of treachery which had also been brought against him.

Sure of speedy acquittal, — for he was the soul of honour, — Romont quietly allowed himself to be led away to a dungeon, where he beguiled the weary hours by long day-dreams, and by composing and singing tender love-songs in praise of the fair Elizabeth.

In the meantime, Charles led the Stein family to his own camp, where he assigned them sumptuous tents, and surrounded them with all manner of graceful attentions. But in spite of all his efforts to win their confidence, Stein and his wife could not help suspecting he was not so good and true as he would fain appear. For this reason they both watched carefully over their daughter, and the Duke could not secure a moment's private intercourse with her, although he frequently tried to do so.

This watchfulness vexed Charles greatly; for while he loved the girl, he had no intention of marrying her, but he knew her parents would detect his evil intentions should he approach her through them.

One day, he accidentally learned that Romont managed to send love-songs to the fair Elizabeth, and that her parents unconsciously encouraged her secret passion for the young prisoner by speaking of him in terms of the highest praise. Thinking he might perchance win Elizabeth by working upon her fears for Romont's safety, the Duke now informed Stein that he would forgive and release the prisoner, provided Elizabeth interceded in his behalf, and if he were allowed to make sure of her real sentiments in a private interview.

Although loath to lose sight of his daughter even for a minute, Stein felt too deeply in Romont's debt to refuse this apparently simple request, and himself conducted Elizabeth to the Duke's tent, where he bade her enter while he mounted guard at the door.

The timid Elizabeth therefore presented herself alone before Charles, who gently reassured her, and then explained that if she would only consent to be his, Romont should be released, but that if she refused, the young man should be put to death.

At first the virtuous Elizabeth could not credit her ears, but when the Duke drew near as if to clasp her in his arms, she fled to her father crying, —

"Take me away, father! The poor prisoner we love will have to die, but I know he would rather lose his life than see me dishonoured!"

Stein gnashed his teeth on hearing these

words, which more than confirmed his darkest suspicions; and while he gently led his weeping daughter back to her mother, he tried to plan how best to avenge this deadly insult.

In the meantime, the Duke feverishly paced his tent, and calling for his confidant asked him what course he could pursue to recover the maiden's confidence and still attain his evil ends. This man, whose task it was to gratify the Duke's passions, now artfully suggested that Charles should declare he had merely wished to test Elizabeth's virtue, and should propose to her parents that she marry Romont without delay. Then, under pretext of sparing the latter the hard duty of fighting against his wife's people, Charles was to dismiss Romont from the army.

But while he thus openly posed as the young people's friend and benefactor, one of his emissaries was to persuade a few of the camp followers that Romont was a traitor, and instigate them to create a disturbance when the bridal party left the church. In the midst of the confusion a hired assassin could easily kill Romont; and the Duke, in pretending to avenge his death and protect Elizabeth, would gain possession of his vast estates and of his young widow, who would then be at his mercy.

This artful plan so pleased Charles that he immediately hastened to the Steins' tent, where he played his part with such consummate skill that they believed all he said, and joyfully consented to their daughter's immediate marriage.

The preparations were speedily made, and the nuptials solemnised ; but as the little procession left the church, Stein and the Duke were detained for a moment by a man with a petition.

Romont, proudly leading his peerless young bride, on whose bosom sparkled the famous diamond, suddenly found himself surrounded by a brawling troop of soldiers, who angrily shook their fists at him and denounced him as a traitor.   Before he could speak one word in his own defence, the hired assassin sprang forward with raised dagger, crying, " Die, thou traitor ! "

Just then Elizabeth sprang forward, and the sharp blade had to pass through her slender body before it could touch Romont. A scene of indescribable confusion ensued ; but although Romont swiftly carried his dying bride into her mother's tent, where every care was lavished upon her, she lived only long enough to whisper, " I die happy since I could save you, beloved ! " and gently breathed her last.

When the fatal truth dawned upon the frantic bridegroom, he fell fainting across his dead bride ; and it was only then that they discovered that he too had been wounded, for his doublet was drenched with blood. Nobly forgetting her own sorrow to minister to her husband's saviour, the Lady of Stein nursed Romont so carefully that in spite of his longing to follow Elizabeth's pure spirit into the better land, he was soon restored to health. But he never forgot his bride, and when her parents ultimately died, he left his own country to take up his abode in a foreign land.

As for the Duke, he was sorely punished for all his crimes. Not only did he lose Elizabeth, whom he passionately loved ; but a few days after her death he was defeated by her countrymen at the battle of Grandson. Such was the fury of that Swiss onslaught, that Charles would have fallen into their hands had not his fleet steed swiftly carried him out of their reach. A few months later he suffered a second crushing defeat at their hands at Morat ; and he was slain near Nancy, in the following year, while trying to escape from his Swiss foes for the third and last time.

FRIBOURG

THE city of Fribourg, capital of the canton
of the same name, is picturesquely situated on a rocky height almost surrounded by
the Sarine, one of the tributaries of the Aare.
A mediæval town, it boasts of many interesting
relics, while in its cathedral stands the great
modern organ known the world over.

When Charles the Bold experienced his
second appalling defeat at Morat, in 1476, one
of the Swiss soldiers volunteered to carry the
joyful tidings to Fribourg, his native city. Although he had fought bravely and was very
weary after his almost superhuman efforts, he
snatched a green twig from a neighbouring lime-
tree, stuck it in his hat so that his people could
see from afar this sign of victory, and quickly
started for home. Tradition claims that he ran
every step of the way; the fact is, he reached
the city so exhausted that he sank down lifeless
as soon as the one word " Victory " had escaped
from his parched lips.

His fellow-citizens were so proud of this
victory, and of the messenger who brought the

news so quickly to them, that they planted the lime twig on the very spot where he had fallen. There it throve and grew, until it is now a mighty tree, with a boll fourteen feet in circumference ; and it still serves as a green monument of this famous triumph of the Swiss army.

The whole valley of the Sarine and its tributaries is most picturesque, and the soil so fertile that it supports countless heads of the finest cattle in the world. After passing the quaint little mediæval town of Romont, with its old castle and fortifications, you come to a hill in the middle of the Sarine valley on which rises the famous castle of Gruyère, recently restored, and now one of the most beautiful show places in Switzerland.

The view from Gruyère is most charming, and includes not only the winding course of the Sarine, and the green hills dotted with the herds, — which furnish the renowned Swiss or Gruyère cheese, — but beyond rise rocky pine-clad mountains, the most important of which is the Moléson.

The founding of the castle of Gruyère is attributed to Gruerius, a captain in the Thebaid legion, who, escaping martyrdom in the days of Diocletian, fled into the mountains. After threading his way through the dense forests which then clothed these grassy hills, he finally reached the point where the castle now stands. There, helped by other fugitive Christians, he began to clear away the primeval forest, and founded the castle and town which bear his name.

Gruyère thus became the cradle of a new race, which, constantly increasing in wealth and power, soon ruled over a vast extent of land peopled by many vassals. The Counts of Gruyère were in general good masters; and the land, carefully tilled by their dependants, grew more and more productive, until many villages dotted the country, while the tinkle of cow-bells was heard for miles around.

In the days of the Crusades, many knights passed this castle on their way to the Holy Land; and the Counts of Gruyère, assuming the cross too, joined them with the fatalistic cry, " Go we must, return who may!" (S'agit d'aller, reviendra qui pourra!")

In spite of their wealth and extensive possessions, the Counts of Gruyère were none too well informed, for we are told they naïvely asked their companions whether the sea they had to cross on their way to Palestine could possibly be as large as the stretch of water

they had seen in making a pilgrimage to the
shrine of Our Lady of Lucerne.

Toward the end of the fourteenth century,
Margaret, Countess of Gruyère, was very sad,
because, although she had already been married
several years, Providence had not yet vouchsafed her a child. In her anxiety to obtain
offspring, this fair Countess consulted the as-
trologers and other fortune-tellers who visited
the castle; but as their promises afforded her
very little satisfaction, she soon resorted to
pilgrimages, fasting, and long seasons of fervent prayer.

All the pilgrims who stopped at the castle, on
their way to and from the shrines at Einsiedlen
and Lucerne, were entertained with the utmost
hospitality at Gruyère, and when they departed
the Countess invariably loaded them with gifts,
gently begging them to intercede for her when
they reached the goal of their pilgrimage.

Garbed like a nun, in the plainest of homespun dresses, the Countess diligently visited the
poor and sick, helped the needy, and was so
good and charitable to all that she was revered
throughout the country like a saint. Besides,
every night and morning, she spent hours on her
knees in the castle chapel, imploring the Virgin
and all the saints to grant her her heart's desire.

One evening, when twilight was fast merging into darkness, she still lingered there on her knees, weeping bitterly because hitherto all her prayers had remained unanswered. Absorbed in sorrowful thoughts, and uttering broken words of supplication between her sobs, the Countess failed to notice the entrance of a lame beggar who had often been the recipient of her bounty.

The sound of suppressed weeping and convulsive prayer soon attracted the beggar's attention, and peering through the gloom, — which the taper burning on the altar only seemed to intensify, — he soon descried a woman clad in rough homespun. Lame Hans, whose sorest trial was an occasional lack of food, immediately concluded that this poor woman must be needy, and catching the word "children," he hastily drew some coarse bread and cheese out of his wallet, and laid it beside her, saying, —

"This is all I have, my poor woman, but the Holy Virgin's blessing resting upon it will enable it to dry your tears."

Then, before the astonished Countess could say a word, the lame man hobbled off; and although he went to bed hungry, he felt a warm glow in the region of his heart whenever he pictured the zest with which the hungry children would devour his bread and cheese.

The Countess came out of the chapel a few moments after Hans, and as she returned to her apartments her servants marvelled at the radiant expression of her face, although it bore marks of recent tears. They were still more surprised when they saw her come forth in her richest apparel to welcome her husband and his friends on their return from the chase. Their amazement was shared by the hunters, who gazed with unconcealed wonder at the hostess whom they had left in the morning pale, silent, and dejected, but who now seemed radiant with life and hope.

Her unwonted vivacity charmed both husband and guests; and when toward the end of the evening meal she begged leave to lay before them a new dish, they all received the proposal with joyful acclamations. At a sign from the fair châtelaine, her aged nurse and favourite page then brought in two covered silver dishes, which they gravely set before their master.

All eyes were riveted on these vessels when the Count of Gruyère simultaneously raised both covers; and his expression of disappointment was mirrored on every face, when instead of choice dainties nothing was seen but the coarse bread and cheese of the peasant population. Interrogative glances were therefore soon directed to the Countess, who with charming grace and simplicity related her adventure in the chapel and repeated the lame beggar's words. She concluded by saying that she now believed her prayers would be answered, and begged all present to partake with her of the food which had come to her in such a strange way. Touched by the tale she told, one and all solemnly ate the bread and cheese she gave them ; but her old nurse laid her share carefully aside, saying she would partake of it only when her mistress's dearest wish had been fulfilled.

Then the castle chaplain arose, filled all the beakers with wine, blessed them as solemnly as if he were about to celebrate a communion service, and all drank to the health of the gracious Countess and the speedy coming of a son and heir to the castle of Gruyère.

Within a year from that day the Stork brought a beautiful boy to the Countess, and at his christening feast many noble guests merrily drank his health. The Countess, radiant with happiness, bestowed bountiful alms upon all the poor, giving lame Hans a new suit of clothes, and a pension to prevent his ever feeling the pangs of hunger again.

In the midst of this feast the old nurse came

in and solemnly ate her carefully treasured share of Hans's bread and cheese. Then she made a deep curtsey to her mistress, saying, —

" Gracious Lady, you see it is just as I always told you. To the one who gives freely, much will be given. May God preserve you and your husband and grant your son a long, happy, and useful life at Gruyère ! "

FROM the castle and town of Gruyère one can enjoy a fine view of the Moléson, the highest peak in that region, from whose summit can be seen the Lake of Geneva with Mont Blanc, the Dent du Midi, and the Diablerets to the south. West and east are the Jura and Titlis mountains, while to the north extends the fertile valley of the Sarine.

Here on the Moléson, as well as on most mountain pastures in Switzerland, you can often hear the famous Ranz des Vaches, Kuhreihen, or musical call, which the cattle no sooner hear than they crowd around their herdsmen.

This melody, repeated by the echoes, and accompanied by the ripple and splash of running waters, the tintinnabulations of cow-bells, and the lowing of the kine, has a peculiar charm for all who hear it, and in words runs about as follows : —

> "The herdsmen of the Colombettes
> At the dawn of day have risen;
>   Ha, ah! ha, ah!
> Cows, cows, to the milking come!
> Come here, all of you.
> White ones and black ones,
> Red and brindled,
> Young ones, old ones,
> Under this oak-tree,
> Where I will milk you;
> Under this poplar,
> Where I will drain you!
> Cows, cows! to the milking come!"[1]

The Moléson was long the favourite field of the chamois-hunters in Fribourg. One of these men having been overtaken by darkness high up on the mountain, once sought refuge in a deserted herdsmen's hut. Drawing near it, he was surprised to hear the tinkle of bells, the lowing and stamping of cattle, and the voices of herdsmen, for he knew the cows had already left the high pastures. Entering the hut, he was further amazed to see four queer, wizened-looking men, whose thumb and first and second fingers were missing. Besides, one of these men was lame, the second hunchbacked, the third had but one eye, and the fourth was apparently a leper.

[1] Poems of Places — Switzerland: Longfellow.

These men signed to him to take a seat near the fire, where they were busy making green cheese, of which, however, they had already a large store in the hut.

The hunchback herdsman offered the guest bread and meat which looked so unpalatable that the hunter took but one mouthful and set the food aside, muttering that they must have forgotten the salt when preparing it. This remark so incensed his hosts that they began to gnash their teeth, and came toward him making such threatening gestures that in sudden terror the hunter made a sign of the cross. At that moment herdsmen, cheese, cows, and fire vanished, and the chamois-hunter found himself alone in the deserted hut.

But when he told his night adventure at home, he learned that a small piece of meat had been cut out of the left hind quarter of his best cow. One of the oldest inhabitants of the village, moreover, informed him that the men whom he had seen were wicked herdsmen, who had neglected their duties while in the flesh, and had besides been guilty of perjury. In punishment for their wickedness, they had not only lost the three fingers upheld in taking an oath, but were condemned to atone for past laziness by working hard every night.

LEGENDS OF NEUCHÂTEL

A YOUNGER son of one the Counts of
Neutchâtel, wishing to found a family of
his own, went to settle in 1155 in the picturesque
Val de Ruz in the Jura mountains. Here he
selected a tall and jagged rock, washed by the
Seyon, as the site of his new stronghold, the
Castle of Vallangin. Owing to its position, it
was almost impregnable ; but it was a very dismal
abode, for the heights of Chaumont at the
south overshadowed it, cutting off much sunlight, while the dense pine forests around it did
not tend to lessen the gloom.

The Val de Ruz was so fertile, however, that
the lords of Vallangin soon grew rich and powerful, ruling wisely over the many peasants who
came to settle there under their protection.
At the end of the thirteenth century their
vassals already numbered many thousands, and
included all classes of society.

Rollin, lord of Vallangin, was but sixteen years
of age, when two of his most powerful vassals
renounced their allegiance to him and prepared

to despoil him of his property. With that end
in view, they armed their retainers and sallied
forth to attack their young master. The friends
of the latter, however, getting wind of this plot,
hastily assembled the noblemen, clergy, and
peasants who were still faithful to their lord,
and consulting with them took active measures
to meet and conquer the foe. Young Rollin
himself, supported by the lords of Neuchâtel,
of Colombiers, and of Vauxtravers, set out at
the head of his army, and meeting the two faithless lords on the plain of Coffrane, defeated their
forces in pitched battle, and secured the persons
of the recreant vassals.

Many men perished on both sides in this
encounter; and hundreds of years later, a staff
of command lost in this battle was ploughed up
by a farmer and placed in the Museum of Neuchâtel, where it is carefully preserved as a relic
of the fight.

Rollin, having seized the faithless vassals,
had them brought before him, and sternly informed them that in his anger at hearing of their
treachery, he had vowed nothing short of two
heads would ever satisfy him. At these words
the guilty lords trembled and grew pale, for
they felt their last hour was near. Their despair
was such that when Rollin bade them reveal

the place where they had concealed their treasures, they offered no resistance, but meekly obeyed. Before long, therefore, two huge heaps of silver lay at Rollin's feet. He gazed at them a few moments in silence, then addressed the culprits, saying:

" I swore I would have two heads, and this solemn vow cannot be recalled. But, as I have never yet sentenced a guilty man to death, I am loath to shed your blood. I will therefore spare you, on condition that two silver heads be cast from this metal, to take the place of those which you have forfeited, but which I allow you to retain. You shall also recover your freedom and go home in peace, but I hereby warn you that should you ever prove faithless again it will be bloody and not bloodless heads which I will claim! "

The delinquent lords, happy to escape their death sentence, solemnly presented two heavy silver heads to the young lord of Vallangin. These were placed by his order on the high altar of the collegiate church at Neuchâtel, where they remained until the days of the Reformation, when an ignorant iconoclast, deeming them idols, removed them from the altar. Since then no trace of the silver busts has been seen.

EARLY in the fourteenth century, some of the vassals of the lord of Vallangin went to settle in the lovely valleys of the Jura Mountains, where, joined by a few families from Burgundy, they founded Le Locle and La Chaux-de-Fonds. These two colonies speedily increased in numbers and wealth, and the towns thus founded are now important centres for the manufacture of watches and jewelry.

Many of the people of the Canton of Neuchâtel having turned Protestant, Wilhelmine of Bergy, grandmother of one of the lords of Vallangin, a stanch Catholic, sadly forsook the castle which she had entered as a happy young bride, to go and live like a hermit in the village of Gezard, which was her dowry.

This lady, already eighty years of age, was lamed by gout and quite feeble, but she nevertheless took great interest in the peasants around her, whom she often visited and frequently helped by her good advice.

One day, sitting among the women of the village who were diligently spinning, she heard them comment bitterly upon their sad lot. saying it was very hard that among all the fields they tilled, there was not a single acre which they could call their very own and which was entirely free from taxation.

Emboldened by the kindly interest the old lady showed in their remarks. they finally ventured to beg her to give them part of her land, to have and to hold without being asked for tithes or rent in exchange. Wilhelmine, who could not dispose of the land otherwise, then said :

" My good women. your request shall be granted. You shall have one half of the land which I can walk around in one day." Saying these words. the old lady painfully rose from her seat, and tottered slowly back to her humble dwelling.

The peasant women, whose hearts had swelled with joy at her first words, but whose hopes had been shattered by the conclusion of her speech, sadly watched her limp out of sight, and then murmured regretfully,—

" The poor mistress is so old and weak, that with the best intentions in the world, she will hardly be able to creep around a single acre !"

Early the next morning. while darkness yet veiled the landscape, and the nightingale's song still pulsated in the quiet air. Wilhelmine of Bergy painfully rose from her couch, and set out on her self-appointed journey, supported on one side by a trusty staff and on the other by a strong young servant maid.

The two women slowly crept out into the darkness, and wandering along the dewy meadows saw the night gradually make way before the first gleams of silvery light. Then they beheld the mountain tops change from blue to silver gray, then turn dazzling white, and suddenly blush and glow beneath the first rays of the rising sun.

The larks rose straight up into the blue, singing their triumphant morning hymn; the bees and butterflies hovered around them, but all the lovely sights and sounds of early morn could not beguile the old lady to take even a moment's rest, and she hobbled bravely on. The peasants, rising from their hard beds to partake of frugal fare before beginning a long day's work, stared in speechless amazement at their aged mistress, already well on her way, and gazed anxiously at the feeble form, wondering how long her strength and energy would last.

All through the bright morning hours, Wilhelmine plodded on without a pause; and it was only when the sun stood directly overhead, that she stopped for a moment under a tree to partake of food and of strengthening drink. Then, while the peasants stretched out in the cool shade to enjoy their midday rest, the old lady again stepped out into the quivering sunshine to continue her task. All through the glowing heat of afternoon, and long after the sun had set and the shades of evening had fallen, Wilhelmine crept on with faltering steps and ebbing strength, but with undiminished energy and determination. Darkness had long set in when she finally reached the village once more, and entering a hut where burned a small rushlight, and where the people had assembled by her order, she cried in weak but joyful accents, —

" My children. I have walked around a thousand acres ! Five hundred of these belong to you, free from all taxes from this time forth. Do not blame me if your share is somewhat small, for I have done all I could to help you, but alas ! although my spirit is willing, my aged feet could carry me no farther."

Having said these words, old Wilhelmine tottered back to her own house, where she lay down so exhausted that she never found the strength to rise from her bed again. But the people whom she had benefited never ceased to be grateful to her ; and when she died, in 1543, six years after this wonderful walk, they mournfully followed her to her last resting-place, shedding abundant tears while softly reminding each other of the many steps taken in their behalf by her weary old feet.

UNTIL the end of the eighteenth century, the city of Neuchâtel boasted a ghost whose apparition was the invariable precursor of a conflagration in town. Shortly before any signs of fire were perceptible, this spectral old woman passed swiftly along the streets, frantically wringing a cloth all dripping with blood until she vanished in a lurid mist in the direction of the lake.

No one now living remembers ever having seen this ghost, but old people in Neuchâtel solemnly aver that the woman was frequently seen by their ancestors, and that a fire always broke out shortly after her visit. They add that the ghost was the unfortunate widow of Walter, Count of Rochefort, publicly accused of forgery, and beheaded, in 1412, on the shores of the lake, on the very spot where the wraith always melted away in a crimson cloud. It is said that the Count's widow, having secured his blood-stained shirt, constantly exhibited it to her sons, urging them to avenge their father, who, according to her assertions, had been wrongfully accused, and condemned without sufficient proof of guilt.

The implacable widow finally prevailed upon these young men to take a fearful revenge by secretly setting fire to the city; and it is a

fact that Neuchâtel was almost destroyed by
what is known as the great conflagration of
1450. Since then, either through remorse or
to parade her spite, the old woman's spectre
heralded every conflagration, until, weary of
destruction, or frightened away by effective
modern methods of fighting fires. she ceased
to haunt the city and frighten the inhabitants.

D. J. RICHARD started the manufacture of
watches in Le Locle and La Chaux-de-Fonds,
but the principal legend relating to that industry refers to Jacques Droz, the clever inventor
of mechanical clocks, of music boxes, and of a
writing automaton.

We are told that in the eighteenth century,
the King of Spain once came to La Chaux-de-
Fonds, and having heard of Jacques Droz's
clever contrivances, went with his suite to visit
the inventor's workshop. There the King examined everything, and was particularly charmed
by a clock upon which stood figures of a negro,
a shepherd, and a dog. Whenever the clock
struck, the shepherd played a soft air upon his
pipe, while his dog frisked joyfully around him.

This artistic contrivance so delighted both
King and courtiers, that one and all loudly expressed their wonder and admiration. Jacques

Droz listened quietly to their exclamations, then turning to the King, he smilingly informed him that the tiny dog was the faithful guardian of his master's property, as could readily be seen if any one attempted to lay hands upon the apples in a basket at the shepherd's feet.

The King, wishing to test the dog's watchfulness, now attempted to abstract an apple, but no sooner had he touched it than the mechanical dog began to bark with such fury that the royal pet hound, springing forward, answered him. The monarch, startled by this unexpected development, stepped back in amazement, while his suite fled, making repeated signs of the cross. None of the Spanish grandees, with the exception of the minister of the navy, remained in the shop, so when the King had recovered from his momentary fright, he laughingly bade that official ask the negro what time it was, adding that after the wonders they had seen, it would not surprise him in the least to hear the darky talk. The minister, therefore, politely inquired the time of day, but as the question was put in Spanish, he received no reply until Jacques Droz suggested that he should repeat it in French, for the negro understood no other tongue.

The minister therefore translated his question

with a somewhat sceptical smile, but when the negro courteously answered: "Messieurs, il est trois heures moins un quart!" (Gentlemen, it is a quarter of three"), he too bolted from the room in terror, crying that the clock must be the work of the Evil One himself!

The legend claims that the King of Spain purchased this wonderful piece of mechanism, but we are told that Jacques Droz merely constructed musical clocks for him. The Spaniards, however, were not the only ones who fancied the watchmaker had made a pact with Satan, for his own countrymen used to look askance at him, and frequently averred that he was a sorcerer.

THE watchmaking industry has long been the great source of gain in western Switzerland, and clocks and watches are shipped from there to all parts of the world. The valleys of Le Locle and La Chaux-de-Fonds being very near the frontier, watches and jewelry are constantly smuggled into France over the mountain paths to avoid paying duty upon them.

In the days of post chaises, this smuggling assumed such proportions that the chief of the French police determined to make a special effort to check it. He therefore journeyed in person to Switzerland, and visiting one of the largest manufactories, selected a case full of fine watches. He then bargained with the manufacturer to pay for the goods only on condition that they were delivered free from duty at a certain address in Paris, and solicitously inquired whether the dealer thought he could pass them across the boundary safely? The merchant smilingly answered that the job presented no insurmountable difficulties, and took leave of his customer, promising that the watches should reach Paris as quickly as he did.

The chief of police, delighted with this answer, went back to the inn, where he gave orders to prepare for immediate departure. Seated in his carriage and rolling rapidly homeward, he congratulated himself upon the clever way in which he had managed ; for all the custom-house officers had been duly warned to guard the frontier with special care, as a large number of watches were to be smuggled over within the next twenty-four hours. Their zeal had further been stimulated by the promise of a large reward should they secure watches and lawbreaker, while speedy punishment was to be the lot of any man who allowed them to escape.

At the frontier. the chief of police made a short halt, and thrusting his head out of the

carriage window, again admonished the officer
there to be very vigilant. The latter, promptly
recognising his superior, confidently answered
that not a squirrel should cross the frontier unseen, for all along the line were posted men
eager to secure the promised reward.

Satisfied by this assurance, the chief of police
now gave orders to drive on, and journeyed
straight to Paris, stopping on his way only
long enough to change horses or partake of
hasty meals.

When he entered his own house, although
worn out by the long and fatiguing journey,
his first question was whether a parcel had
arrived for him from Switzerland. His servants promptly denied having seen anything of
the sort, so the chief of police threw himself
down in an armchair, gleefully exclaiming:
"Then my men have managed to intercept it
at the frontier, and we will make such an
example of the smugglers that none will venture to continue this business!"

His satisfaction did not last long, however,
for, upon entering his bedroom, he saw resting
upon the top of the rest of his luggage a case,
which, upon investigation, was found to contain the very watches he had purchased in
Switzerland.

In his anger, the chief of police hotly inquired of his servants how the parcel had come there ; but none could give him any information, further than that it had probably been brought in without their notice by one of the men called to attend to his luggage.

The chief of police, angrier than ever, wrote scathing letters to all the custom-house officers, who one and all declared they were ready to stake their lives and reputations that no one, except himself, had crossed the frontier without being subjected to a thorough search.

Still hoping to secure the man who had delivered the parcel in Paris, and of reaching the smugglers through him, the chief of police now sent for his coachman, to ask him whether he had seen any one carry the case of watches into his house. To his amazement the coachman immediately replied, —

" Indeed I did. I gave it to the man myself, and was very glad to see the last of it, I can tell you ! "

This answer astounded his master, who, upon asking for an explanation, learned that while the coachman was preparing the carriage for departure in the inn yard at La Chaux-de-Fonds, one of the waiters had suddenly appeared with a box, saying his master wished him to stow it away under his seat and keep it safely out of sight of every one until they reached Paris. He added that the case contained articles of great value which the chief feared might else fall into the hands of highwaymen, who of course would not dream of looking under the coachman's seat for anything but oats. Thus cautioned, the coachman had carefully hidden the box away; but throughout the journey he had refused to lose sight of the carriage for an instant, lest his master's secret should be discovered, and his property stolen.

On receiving this explanation, the chief of police made a wry face, for he now perceived how cleverly he had been outwitted by the watchmaker. The latter, having discovered his customer's identity in some mysterious way, had defeated his purpose by bribing one of the inn waiters to give the box to the coachman, thus making the chief of police unconsciously smuggle his own goods across the frontier!

ANOTHER story runs that a Swiss naturalist often crossed the frontier at Pontarlier, where he was greatly annoyed by a cross and overzealous French custom-house officer. The latter, for some inscrutable reason, had conceived an intense dislike to the Swiss savant, whose luggage he always examined with exaggerated care, although the naturalist was well known as a man of unimpeachable integrity.

Exasperated by this rude treatment, the naturalist finally determined to give this disagreeable official a lesson which he would not be likely to forget in a hurry. The next time he stopped at Pontarlier, therefore, besides his usual baggage, he had a tightly closed box, which he handled with special care.

In answer to the customary question, he truthfully swore he had no dutiable goods with him, but the custom-house officer, who had singled him out as his victim, gruffly demanded his keys and proceeded to turn his trunk topsy turvy as usual. To his evident chagrin, not the tiniest object upon which he could exact payment was forthcoming, but leaving the owner to rearrange his tumbled garments as best he might, the officer took up the box, shook it hard, and asked what it contained.

"Natural history specimens," quietly answered the naturalist.

This reply elicited a contemptuous snort from the officer, who declared such a statement must be verified. The naturalist then protested vehemently, swore it contained nothing contraband, and finally seeing that he could not prevent the opening of the box, angrily cried, —

"Very well! Open the box if you choose, but don't blame me for the consequences!" and marched out of the office where the discussion had taken place, slamming the door behind him with marked emphasis.

Left alone, the officer, armed with chisel and hammer, proceeded to tear off the cover of the box, out of which squirmed and tumbled a number of small snakes.

With a wild cry of terror, the custom-house officer rushed out of the office, crying, "Snakes, snakes!" but as he was often tipsy, or "lost his way in his master's vineyard," — as the local saying goes, — his companions would not believe him, and fancied he was the victim of a delusion natural to a man of his intemperate habits.

But one of his comrades venturing boldly into the office to convince him of his mistake, came out again precipitately, crying that snakes were really crawling all over the floor! The naturalist now stepped forward, calmly offered to replace the reptiles — which were perfectly harmless — in their box, and added that he had warned the officer not to tamper with natural history specimens.

After that, the custom-house officers at Pontarlier were particularly careful how they handled this savant's luggage, and never again did they venture to raise the cover of any box when he told them that it contained materials for his collections.

BERN

THE little city of Erlach, or Cerlier, on the Lake of Bienne, is romantically situated at the foot of the Jolimont, on which stand great rocks known as the Devil's Burden. We are told that his Infernal Highness brought these stones hither to crush the Christians at the foot of the mountain. But, turned aside by the hand of God, the blocks fell where they could do no damage, and now serve as picturesque features in the landscape.

The castle of Erlach, founded in 1100 by a bishop of Basel, was entrusted to the care of a governor, or bailiff. who made ruthless demands upon the time and strength of his master's vassals. No servant was ever strong and diligent enough to suit him; and when a tall foreigner came to offer his services, the bailiff, noting his well-developed muscles, immediately said he would engage him provided he could lift the huge rock which stood at the castle gate.

Picking up the stone with the utmost ease, the newcomer tossed it up as if it were a mere pebble, although its weight was such that it sank deep into the ground on the spot where it fell. This proof of strength fully satisfied the bailiff, who at first treated his new servant quite fairly. But as time went on, he exacted more and more, and once bade him take four horses and bring back to the castle a load of wood which twelve horses could not have drawn without great effort.

The muscular servant nevertheless set out undaunted to fulfil this task, and finding one pair of horses inclined to balk, unharnessed them, tied them to the tail of the cart, and taking their place, pulled so vigorously that the load safely reached the foot of the hill leading to the castle. There, however, the second pair of horses stopped short, and refused to advance another step. The servant quickly unharnessed these, too, bound them on top of the wood, and single-handed drew wood, wagon, and horses up the hill, although the load was so heavy that the deep ruts it made in the rock road can still be seen to this day.

When the bailiff beheld this new and startling proof of great strength, he was duly awed, and fearing the servant might prove troublesome some day, determined to get rid of him. With that purpose in view, he ordered a well dug, and when it was quite deep, made his men throw a huge stone down upon the strong servant's head. To the general surprise, this man tossed the stone up out of the well again, muttering. "Don't throw any more sand down into my eyes, or I 'll get mad."

But looking up just then, he caught such an evil expression in the bailiff's eyes that he was seized with a sudden fit of blind rage. Scrambling out of the hole. he pursued the conscience-stricken bailiff into the castle ; and as neither man nor master were ever seen again, people suppose that the strong servant must have been an emissary of Satan, sent to carry their cruel master off to Hades, to receive due punishment for all his crimes.

On the way from Basel to Bern, the train passes through a long tunnel piercing a hill upon which stand the ruins of Castle Grimmenstein. This was once the home of so enthusiastic a hunter, that he even broke the Sabbath to indulge in his favourite sport. His wife, a gentle and pious soul, once vainly besought him not to desecrate a particularly holy day of rest, but he nevertheless sallied forth, and after a long search came across a doe with its young.

Although this gentle animal bravely tried to defend her offspring. the cruel hunter slew them all one after another. But, just as the doe breathed her last, a giant sprang out of the ground, shook his fist vehemently at the Sabbath-breaker, and exclaiming that the harmless animals were already avenged, vanished with them underground!

The lord of Grimmenstein, awed in spite of himself by these mysterious words and by the sudden disappearance of the quarry he had slain, gave up all thought of further hunting for that day and rode slowly home. But when he entered his wife's apartment, he found her and his children dying from the very wounds he had inflicted upon the gentle doe and her young.

Ever since then, when war or pestilence threaten the land, the lord of Grimmenstein rises from his grave, blows a resonant blast upon his hunting-horn, and again sets out to range through woods and valleys in quest of game.

Besides this hunter and Sabbath-breaker, almost every valley and hillside in Switzerland is said to be visited at times by some similar wraith, sweeping by on the wings of the wind. But the apparition which makes the most noise and causes most damage is undoubtedly that of Odin, the Wild Huntsman himself, who often rushes through the land with all his ghostly train of heathen deities.[1]

[1] See the author's "Myths of Northern Lands."

THE WILD HUNT.

AFTER passing through the Wynigen tunnel, the train soon comes to Burgdorf, an ancient and picturesque little city, with an old castle in which Pestalozzi established a school toward the end of the eighteenth century.

Tradition relates that dense forests once covered all this region, which was infested by wild beasts of all kinds, not omitting an immense, fire-breathing dragon, which had its abode in a cave in the hill on which Burgdorf castle now stands.

Sintram and Baltram, the two sons of the Duke of Lenzburg, once penetrated into this wilderness in pursuit of game, and discovering the trail of this dragon, resolved to track him into his lair and rid the country of such a pest. But when they drew near the mouth of the cave, the dragon suddenly darted forth, and seizing Baltram, swallowed him at one gulp! At this sight Sintram boldly dismounted, drew his sword, and attacked the monster with such fury that he finally laid him low. Then, slitting him open, he had the good fortune to find his brother still alive and quite unharmed, thanks to the strong armour he wore.

The brothers were so proud of their victory over the monster, and so grateful for their miraculous escape from its teeth and claws, that they built a chapel on this spot, dedicating it to St. Margaret, because she too once met and defeated a dragon. In this chapel they placed a picture representing their fight with the Burgdorf monster, and as they soon founded the town and castle, their name and fame still endures in that section of the country.

In the twelfth century, Burgdorf was the home of Berthold V. of Zähringen, who conquered and brought into subjection the various nobles in the Bernese Oberland. He built Fribourg on his own land, and founded a new city on a rocky height almost entirely surrounded by the Aare. History claims that he called this town Bern, in honour of his favourite hero and ancestor, Dietrich of Bern (Verona).[1] But legend states that, not knowing what name to bestow upon the new city, he decided to call it after the first animal he slew in the chase.

Sallying forth one day, he met and slew some bears (*Bären*), and therefore called the city Bern. It is because the city is popularly supposed to have thus obtained its name, that there is a bear in its shield, and that these animals are conspicuous there in every form. The

---

[1] See the author's " Legends of the Middle Ages."

most famous and imposing bears in Bern are the stone effigies which long stood on either side of the city gates, and which now guard the entrance to the Historical Museum; but the most amusing are undoubtedly the live bears kept in a special pit.

According to some authorities these animals are the descendants of a cub which the Duke of Zähringen brought back from his memorable hunting expedition; according to others of a pair given to the town by René, Duke of Lorraine. Besides, you may also hear it stated that a Swiss soldier brought home a couple of cubs as trophy after the battle of Novarre, in 1513, which were preserved in the city. In 1798, General Brune carried off the Bern bears to the Jardin des Plantes in Paris, and the present bruins are also said to have descended from those or from a pair imported from Russia.

The city of Bern was laid out for the Duke by his henchman von Bubenberg, who, foreseeing its importance, made it twice as large as he was told. The Duke in wrath then demanded what he meant by this disobedience, but von Bubenberg soon proved that he was right, for so many settlers poured into the new place that only a narrow space could be allotted for each

house.　All the buildings were made from the
wood growing within the new city limits, which
gave rise to the distich, —

> " Holz, lass' dich hauen gern,
>   Die Stadt muss heissen Bern."
>   (Wood, let yourself be felled readily,
>   The city must be called Bern.)

Bern became independent soon after its
foundation, bravely withstood two sieges made
by the redoubtable Rudolf von Hapsburg, and
some time after defeating the Burgundian forces
at Laupen, in 1339, joined the Swiss Confederation, of which it is now the head.

In the middle of the fifteenth century, the
citizens began the construction of the beautiful
cathedral, which, owing to lack of funds, remained incomplete for centuries and has only
recently been crowned by its wonderful spire.
In front of this building now stands the eques-
trian statue of Rudolph von Erlach, the hero
of Laupen ; but here, too, once stood a large
wooden statue of St. Christopher.　It was
placed there after a silver communion service
had been stolen from the cathedral, for the people believed that the giant saint would mount
faithful guard over ecclesiastical property.　But
when in spite of his presence there, the com-

munion service again fell a prey to thieves, great indignation was felt in town.

To punish St. Christopher for his lack of vigilance, he was banished to a niche in a tower bearing his name, where, as a further mark of disgrace, and because he stood directly opposite the fountain of David, he was dubbed Goliath. At that time a tradition was current in Bern that when St. Christopher *heard* the town clock strike the noon hour, he invariably rained *weckli* (local rolls) down upon the people. To fix this saying in the minds of a younger generation, a lady of the town ordered a large number of *weckli* cast down upon the waiting school children at the stroke of twelve, one day before the tower was razed and the statue removed. The benevolent woman who played this innocent trick upon the delighted little ones, celebrated her one-hundredth birthday at Bern, in 1897, when the cathedral chimes pealed forth at noon a gay carillon in her honour.

When the quaint Christopher tower was torn down, in the middle of the nineteenth century, the head of the gaudily coloured statue of the saint was removed to the city Museum, where it now forms part of a collection of local antiquities.

South of the Cathedral, and extending all

along one side of the building, is a beautiful
broad terrace, commanding a marvellous view
of the whole range of the Bernese Alps. On
this shady place stands a fine statue of the
founder of the city, with Bruin as his shield-
bearer. At the edge of the terrace, set deep
in the wall, is a tablet commemorating the miraculous escape of a student, whose frightened
horse vaulted over the parapet in 1654. Theo-
bald Weinzäpfli, for such was the student's
name, not only survived the fall which killed his
steed, but became pastor of Kerzerz, where he
died forty years later.

From the terrace, besides the matchless back-
ground of glaciers, there is a fine view of the
pyramidal Niesen, darkly outlined against them,
and of the winding Aare, which passes through
the Lake of Brienz and that of Thun at the foot
of this mountain. At one end of the Lake of
Thun, where the Aare has its outlet, and less
than an hour's railway journey from Bern,
stands the picturesque little city of Thun, with
its ancient castle. At the other extremity, on
a narrow strip of land between the two lakes,
rises Interlaken, the goal of all Swiss tourists.

Legend claims that in the days when St.
Peter was preaching in Rome, he converted

THE OLD ST. CHRISTOPHER TOWER.

there an English traveller, who received in baptism the name of Beatus. Longing to publish the good tidings he had received, this pious man set out from Rome, and preaching as he went, finally came to the shores of the Lake of Thun. There he found a large population of thrifty people still devoted to the Scandinavian religion practised by their ancestors.

The spot was so lovely, and the task awaiting him so urgent, that Beatus resolved to make a prolonged sojourn; but he was so busy caring for souls that he had no time to build himself a hut. He therefore determined to take up his abode in some cave, and searching for one which might answer his purpose, climbed the mountain on the north side of the lake. Far up the slope, he descried a large cavern, which he was about to enter. But he suddenly found himself face to face with a huge dragon, whose eyes were as big and round as cart-wheels, whose claws were as long and as hard as grappling-hooks, and whose long, tapering body and tail were covered with scales so thick that no weapon could pierce them! This monster lashed its tail, opened wide its capacious jaws, and spat forth such a torrent of fire and smoke that Beatus thought his last hour had surely come. Alone and unarmed, resistance was impossible, and as flight would have been equally vain, Beatus commended his soul to God and made a hasty sign of the cross.

At the same moment the monster crept back into its den with a cry of rage and terror; and Beatus, perceiving that it had quailed at the sign of the cross, immediately determined to use so potent a weapon to rid the country of this emissary of Satan. He therefore took up his post at the mouth of the Beatushöhle, where he mounted guard night and day, fasting and praying persistently. The presence of this holy man, the constant sound of fervent supplication, and the sight of the awe-inspiring sign of the cross every time it moved, so worked upon the dragon's nerves, that it exploded on the eighth day, and vanished in a cloud of stinking smoke.

The Evil One having thus departed, Beatus took possession of the cave, which he fitted out to serve as a hermitage. From one of the trees on the bank of the lake, he fashioned a rude skiff, in which he rowed from point to point along the shore, often preaching from his boat as his Master had done on the Sea of Galilee.

By the blessing of God, Beatus' words bore rich fruit, and conversions became so numerous that Satan was alarmed, and determined to make another attempt to kill or drive away the zealous missionary. He therefore stirred up fearful storms every time Beatus left his cave, caused brooks to swell and overflow whenever he tried to cross them, rolled rocks down the mountain to obstruct his pathway, and after many vain trials, succeeded in breaking his oars and making his poor skiff almost useless.

One day, when Beatus came down to the lakeside, he perceived that the waves rose to such a height that it would be impossible for him to cross the lake to officiate at Einigen as he had promised. Loath to disappoint the faithful anxiously awaiting him, Beatus spread out his cloak upon the bank and sat down upon it, hoping that the storm stirred up by the Evil One would soon abate sufficiently to enable him to cross without imminent danger.

While sitting there, inwardly praying, a gust of wind suddenly stole under his outspread cloak ; and a moment later Beatus found himself soaring through the air, high over the tossing lake, and was soon gently deposited on the greensward near the little church. The people welcomed him gladly, listened to his teachings, and practised the Christian virtues so diligently that the place where they assembled for worship was soon known far and wide as Paradise.

The concourse of people there became daily greater, and as Beatus was often busy elsewhere, he bade his disciple Justus take charge of the services whenever he failed to appear at the appointed time. Now, it seems that while Beatus himself was very eloquent, his disciple was extremely prosy and long-winded; and Satan, perceiving this, determined to claim, on the judgment day, the souls of all those who slept through the sermon and thus missed the final benediction. He therefore entered the little church at Einigen one Easter morning, seated himself directly under the pulpit, and spreading out a ram-skin on his lap, prepared to take down the names of all who dozed during the service. Although Beatus was expected to preach on that day, and an unusually large congregation was present, he had not yet appeared when the little bell ceased ringing; so Justus mounted the pulpit and began to expound the Scriptures in his stead.

The place was overcrowded, the weather quite warm; and as the worthy man's teachings were even more uninteresting than usual, one auditor after another nodded and slept. Beatus, who had been detained by a work of mercy, slipped unperceived into the church shortly after the sermon had begun, and seating himself modestly in a corner, lent a reverent and attentive ear to his colleague's halting discourse.

Looking up, however, he suddenly became aware of the fact that the whole congregation was fast asleep, and that the Evil One was jotting down their names with fiendish glee. While Beatus was hesitating whether to be guilty of the sin of disturbing divine service by making a noise which would wake the imprudent sleepers, or whether he should leave their souls in such a dangerous predicament without making an effort to save them, he perceived that the Devil had almost reached the bottom of his ram-skin, and had not space enough left to inscribe all the remaining names.

At that very moment the Devil became aware of the selfsame fact, but, notoriously quick at devising expedients, he immediately seized the skin between his teeth, and began tugging at it with all his might so as to stretch it sufficiently to serve his purpose. In his haste he gave a jerk which, tearing the skin, threw his head backward, hitting the pulpit such a resonant bang that every man, woman, and child in the congregation awoke with a start.

Beatus, the only one who had seen the acci-

dent, disgraced himself by laughing aloud; and
the Devil, perceiving he had defeated his own
ends, flounced angrily out of the church, and
vanished with a yell, while the people sank on
their knees and frantically prayed to be forgiven
for yielding to fatigue.

Beatus, we are told, was duly punished for
laughing in church, for when he again spread
out his mantle, expecting to be wafted across
the lake, as usual, it remained stationary, and
although he ultimately died in the odour of
sanctity and was duly canonised, he ever after
had to resort to ordinary means of transporta-
tion.   The cave in which Beatus dwelt on the
Beatenberg, and which still bears his name,
has been uninhabitable since his day.   From
its mouth now pours forth a noisy stream during
the spring months, and after heavy falls of rain.

MANY steamboats daily furrow the lake over
which St. Beatus was wont to fly on his mantle;
and after passing the romantic town of Ober-
hofen, directly opposite Einigen, where Justus
preached, they come to Spiez, where stands a
tower of the old castle of Strättlingen.   A lord
of that name is said to have been suddenly converted, while out hunting, by the sight of a stag
bearing a luminous crucifix between its wide

antlers. During the Christian persecutions under Hadrian. this Strättlingen took refuge in Burgundy, where he greatly distinguished himself during a quarrel with France.

It seems that the two kings had decided that their difference should be settled by a duel between champions of their selection. The king of France, however, produced a giant so strong that no Burgundian dared meet him ; and when Strättlingen volunteered to fight, the king of Burgundy was duly grateful.

Reaching the lists before his antagonist, Strättlingen sat down to await his coming, which he dreaded so little that he quietly fell asleep. When the giant came, he gazed in angry astonishment at a rival snoring as peacefully five minutes before the redoubtable encounter as if he were merely taking a nap before dinner. Convinced that some miracle lay behind this marvellous composure, the giant gazed at his foe more closely still, and declared himself ready to acknowledge his defeat without striking a blow. because the Archangel Michael stood beside the sleeping champion, ready to battle for him.

In reward for the great victory thus won in his sleep. the Burgundian king gave Strättlingen his daughter's hand in marriage, a large estate on the Lake of Thun, and great treasures. Part of this wealth was employed by Strätt-lingen in erecting the castle which still bears his name, and which long remained in the pos-session of his family.   One of his descendants, Wernhardt von Strättlingen, was known far and wide for his great charity, and when a shivering pilgrim knocked at his gate one cold winter morning, he unhesitatingly bestowed upon him a brand-new cloak and bade him enter and spend the night in the castle.

When morning came, pilgrim and cloak had vanished, and the lady of Strättlingen, who was very economical and far less charitable than her spouse, reproached him bitterly. for wasting such a good cloak upon an ungrateful scamp. Although her scolding was vehement and oft renewed, the husband bore it patiently, and when about to set out on a pilgrimage, parted amicably with her, giving her half his ring and telling her she might marry again at the end of five years, if in the meantime he did not return to claim her by producing the other half of the circlet.

This arrangement made, Strättlingen set out for Garganum, where he had heard that St. Michael, his patron saint, had recently alighted. Arriving there, he had a vision of St. Michael himself, who gave him his blessing.   But on the way home, Strättlingen was cast into a prison in Lombardy, where he languished four whole years. Throughout this long captivity Strättlingen's faith never wavered; and when came the time set for his wife's remarriage should he not return, he fervently prayed that she might be preserved from bigamy.

At that moment the pilgrim appeared in his cell, wrapped in the mantle he had given him, and humbly confessed that he was a demon sent to Strättlingen to entrap him into a reckless act of charity, in hopes that the scolding his wife was sure to administer would cause him to sin. The demon next went on to explain that he was now sent by St. Michael to convey him home. Then he proceeded to carry out the orders he had received from the archangel, and did it so skilfully that a few minutes later the lord of Strättlingen stood at his castle gate, wrapped in the cloak he had given the pilgrim five years before.

Returning thus unexpectedly and unrecognised, Strättlingen perceived that wedding preparations were even then being made. Amid the throng of guests, he stepped up to the table unseen and dropped his half of the ring into his wife's cup. When she raised it to her lips to drink, she found this pledge, and looking eagerly

around her, recognised her husband in his pilgrim's garb and fell upon his neck.   Instead of
a wedding feast, a banquet of reunion was now
held in the great hall at Strättlingen, and as
thank-offering for his miraculous return, the
count built the church of St. Michael at
Einigen.

This church was secretly dedicated by the
archangel himself, who graciously made that
fact known to the noble builder.   The latter is
said to have founded a dozen other churches in
the neighbourhood, besides one large monastery.
After a time, however, he began to pride himself
upon his piety and great gifts to the church, and
in punishment for this sin, fell desperately ill.

During this illness he saw the archangels
Michael, Raphael, and Gabriel wrestling with
the Devil for the possession of his soul.   But
they finally agreed to decide the matter in a
strictly impartial way by weighing Strättlingen's
good and bad deeds in opposite scales.   Held
by one saint and filled by another and by the
Devil, the scales wavered for a moment.   Then
the one containing the virtues seemed inclined
to kick the beam, until St. Michael rested his
hand heavily upon it.   Seeing this, the Devil
slyly clung to the bottom of the scale in which
he was specially interested.   But his black and

claw-like fingers appearing over the edge of the scale, betrayed his stratagem to St. Michael, who, drawing his sword, drove him away.

This curious legend is illustrated by a painting which long graced the church in Lauterbrunnen, and the various legends told above are carefully preserved in the curious chronicle of the church at Einigen.

Opposite Spiez, at the foot of the Ralligenstock, and near the present town of Ralligen, there was once a village named Roll, whose inhabitants were noted all along the lake shore for their selfishness and pride.

One night when the wind was blowing very hard and after it had rained persistently for several days, a little dwarf came into the village, and knocking at every door humbly begged for shelter. All rudely refused to receive him, except an aged couple living at the end of the village. They bade him enter, gave him the best food that they had in the house, and would gladly have let him sleep in their own bed, had he only been willing to tarry with them over night. But the dwarf told them he still had much to do, and bidding them farewell, ran through the place again, crying that it would soon disappear.

Before morning a terrible storm broke, the lightning struck the top of the Ralligenstock, and all at once the awestruck people heard the rumbling sound of a great landslide. Peering hastily out of their window, the charitable couple saw their little guest gliding rapidly down the mountain side on a huge rock, which he seemed to steer like a sled. Guiding this rock close to their hut, he brought it to a sudden standstill there, making it serve as a bulwark for the tiny house where he had been so hospitably entertained. The rest of the earth and stones swept all the other houses and inhabitants of Roll into the lake, in punishment for their pride and lack of hospitality. But we are told that the little cabin so miraculously spared, stood on the very site of the present castle of Ralligen.

On the same side of the Lake of Thun, and not very far from Ralligen, is the charmingly situated town of Merligen. According to somewhat malicious legends, the people there were none too intelligent. They once built a beautiful City Hall, but discovered only too late that they had forgotten to provide any windows, and that it was pitch dark inside. As it was impossible to transact business in utter obscurity, the city council immediately declared light must be brought in without delay, and bade each of the councillors procure a bagful. All therefore betook themselves in a body to a sunny meadow, opened wide their sacks, and when they saw them full of sunlight, closed them tight and bore them off to the City Hall. But although one bagful after another of golden sunshine was carried in there, and all were opened at once, the hall, to their great surprise and disappointment, remained as dark as ever.

There once stood a nut tree close by the lake at Merligen. It bent so far over the water that the people fancied the topmost branches wanted a drink, so they determined to help it reach the water. The chief magistrate climbed the tree, and seizing the highest bough, bade another citizen catch hold of his legs. This done, a third clung to the second, and continuing thus the people formed a living chain which reached down into the lake. The last man now cried, —

"Are you all ready? Shall we pull?"

"No!" cried the chief magistrate, "wait a minute; I want to spit in my hands!"

Saying this, he suddenly let go, and the whole chain of men splashed into the lake, where they were drowned!

At the end of the eighteenth century, after the

French had carried off the treasure of Bern to meet the expenses of the Egyptian war, the other cities decided it might be well to hide or bury their valuables, lest they too should fall into their enemies' hands. The people of Merligen therefore put all their treasures on board a boat, rowed out to the middle of the lake, and sank them in the deepest spot. To make sure, however, that they would be able to find again the exact spot where the valuables were lying, they carefully drew a heavy mark on their boat directly above the sunken treasure. Unfortunately, this streak did not remain on the spot where the treasure was hidden, but to the dismay of the people accompanied them back to Merligen; and it is said no one has ever yet been able to locate these valuables, whose loss is still mourned.

THE strip of land between the lakes of Thun and Brienz is watered by the Aare, which, flowing through both these bodies of water, also serves as a connecting link between them. Interlaken, as its name indicates, is situated between the two lakes.

From the steamboats on the Lake of Brienz, one can see the wooded slopes and charming village of Iseltwald. Here, we are told, you

often hear sounds such as might be produced
by a huge Æolian harp. Sometimes loud, sometimes low, the melancholy, ghost-like melody
quivers softly through the summer air.

Tradition assures us that a huntsman of this
region had his right arm disabled by a stroke
of lightning ; so, taking up his hunting horn, he
wandered from place to place, playing wonderful tunes for a living. His admiring auditors
rewarded him for his music by small gifts,
and all delighted in his constant tunes. Early
in the morning, when the first lark rose to
the sky, the stirring notes of " Awake, my
heart, and sing ! " roused the sleeping inhabitants ; and far into the night gentle reveries
lulled them to sleep. All day long the music
played strong, brisk, helpful accompaniments to
their labours, and when a thief prowled about
their huts at night, ready to seize their property,
a sharp danger signal from the ever-ready horn
pealed through the quiet air.

Every one loved the wandering huntsman, —
no feast or funeral was complete without him,
and wherever he went he invariably met with
an enthusiastic welcome. The time came, however, when the poor man felt his last hour was
near ; and seating himself near the edge of the
lake he played a melodious farewell to life, and

to the land he loved. Then, addressing a lame beggar who had stolen up to listen to his music, he gave him all the money he had, on condition that he would promise to bury him in the Iseltwald.

"But," he added, "be sure to place my beloved hunting horn in my hand. It has been my friend and comforter for many a year; and if the dead can still feel and move, I shall be glad to beguile the dark and lonely hours spent in my grave. There I shall play soft tunes, until released by the peal of Gabriel's trump on the day of judgment, when I, too, shall arise to take part in the grand concert played before the throne of God."

The old huntsman had scarcely finished these words when he died; and true to his promise the beggar laid him to rest at the foot of a mighty oak, with his beloved horn clasped tight in his dead hand. Since then, belated boatmen have often heard a musical call guiding them safely homeward; and the still summer air often pulsates with the sweet, weird melody the huntsman softly plays to himself while waiting to join in the grand Hallelujah Chorus on the judgment day.

AFTER leaving Iseltwald the steamers on the Lake of Brienz stop at the Giessbach, part of

THE GIESSBACH.

which famous falls can be seen from its deck, and thence run on to Brienz, where one can take the train to Meiringen and see the beautiful Reichenbach.

Near the last-named town, on the way to the Hohenstollen, whence a magnificent view is obtainable, one passes the Balisalp, of which the following picturesque legend is told. A shepherd named Res used to tend his cattle here ; and after they were duly cared for every evening, he was wont to take the huge funnel through which he poured his milk into his pans, and reversing it, step out on a projecting ledge of rock to call out a loving good-night to his sweetheart, who spent the summer on the See-alp. Then, when it was too dark to see the place where she stood, he would quietly enter his hut, climb up into the loft, and lying down on his pallet, would sleep soundly until the next day, when his first morning greeting was also shouted to the girl he loved.

One night the herdsman suddenly awoke, and hearing a crackling sound, peered down into the châlet to see what it might be. To his surprise he saw three strange-looking men sitting around a bright fire they had kindled on his hearth, busy making cheese in a giant kettle. The largest of the three kept stirring the milk, the next one brought more to add to it, while the third kept up a bright blaze by adding fuel to the fire from time to time.

Watching these men, the owner of the hut saw the cheesemaker pour a reddish fluid into the kettle. Then the second stepped to the door, and taking a huge horn, began to play a weird melody. Low at first, it gradually roused all the echoes, and had a magical effect, for all the cows came running up to him and soon stood around in a circle as if to listen. This musical performance ended, the third man poured the contents of the huge kettle into three vessels, and the watching herdsman noted with surprise that the liquid in each receptacle was of a different hue.

Just then, the tallest man looked up, and bade the herdsman come down and drink from any vessel he pleased, — explaining that if he partook of the red liquid he would be as strong as a giant and receive one hundred cows; if he tasted of the green, he would have a large fortune; while if he chose the white, he would receive the magic horn and be able to play the weird tune, which, as he had seen, would charm cows as well as men.

The young dairyman had been so enraptured by the music he had heard, that he unhesitatingly snatched the bowl containing the white liquid and took a deep draught. When he set it down again, his strange visitors warmly congratulated him upon his selection, for had he drunk out of either of the other vessels he would surely have died, and centuries would have elapsed before the Alphorn would again have been offered to mankind. This explanation given, the three strangers suddenly vanished, leaving no trace of their presence save the Alphorn, which the young man put to his lips just as the first gleams of light appeared in the east. Then, to his delight, he found he could play as well as the mysterious stranger.

He soon made a second horn just like the one he had received from his night visitors, and taught his beloved to use it. They kept up a lively musical intercourse all summer, although too far apart to hear each other's words. In the autumn they were married, and their descendants inherited their wonderful musical instruments, and still play the peculiar air, which has, as yet, lost none of its primitive charm.

A similar story is told of the Wengernalp, where, however, on the eve of the wedding, the young herdsman's musical call was answered by a ghostly voice announcing the death of his betrothed. The expectant bridegroom was so shocked by these tidings that he dropped his wonderful horn, which was shattered on the rocks below him. Then, maddened by grief, he ranged the mountain, until, in a fit of despair, he committed suicide.

Since then, many imitations have been made of the magic horn, but none has ever reproduced any of its best high notes, and all the present instruments are remarkable for their deep, sad tones, which produce an indescribably mournful impression upon all those who hear them for the first time.

On the way from Meiringen to the famous Rhône glacier, one sees some of the most beautiful and varied scenery in the world. After passing charming points too numerous to mention, the road, which rises rapidly, leads over the barren Grimsel Pass, where stands a famous refuge for poor travellers, the well-known Grimsel Hospice.

A legend claims that in olden times this region blossomed like the rose, and that the highest mountains were as fertile as any valley nestling in a sheltered location at their foot. When Our Lord bade the Wandering Jew[1]

[1] See the author's "Legends of the Virgin and Christ."

begin the never-ending journey for which he is so noted, he immediately set out, and tramping incessantly, started to cross the Alps at the Grimsel. Although constantly urged along by a power he could not resist, Ahasuerus, the Jew, marked the happy people dwelling on the banks of the Aare and the Rhône, and marvelled at the extreme fertility of the pass, where grapes and figs grew in abundance, where no barren spot could be seen, and where mighty oaks covered the tops of mountains now crowned by eternal snows.

The air was mild and balmy, even at the greatest altitude ; and hosts of birds in bright plumage flitted about, twittering and singing in the merriest way. Ahasuerus also noticed that the people were gentle and hospitable, for wherever he asked for food or drink it was quickly granted, and he was warmly invited to tarry with them and rest his weary limbs. This invitation, however, he could not accept ; but hurried on, unconscious of the fact that a blight fell over every place through which he passed ; for the curse laid upon him not only condemned him to move on for ever, but enhanced his punishment by making cold, want, and pestilence follow in his train.

Many years passed by before the Wandering

Jew again found himself near the Alps; but weary as he was, he somewhat quickened his footsteps, hoping to feast his eyes upon the landscape which had so charmed him the first time, and to meet again the warm-hearted people who had been so kind to him once before.

As he drew near the mountains, however, sad forebodings wrung his heart, for they were enveloped in a dense fog, which seemed to him particularly cold and clammy. Hurrying on up the pass, he eagerly looked from side to side, yet saw nothing but dark pines wildly tossing their sombre branches against a gray sky, while ravens and owls flew past him, croaking and hooting. Vines, figs, and oaks had vanished, and the happy people, driven away by the constant windstorms which swept the mountains, had taken refuge in the sheltered valleys. But although all else was changed, the spirit of hospitality still lingered on the heights, for the charcoal-burners gladly shared their meagre supply of coarse food with the Wandering Jew, and warmly invited him to be seated at their campfire.

The Jew, however, had to hasten on; and many long years elapsed before he again trod the Grimsel Pass. For a while he still perceived dark firs and smouldering fires, but it seemed to him that they were much nearer the foot of the mountain than they had been at his second visit. As he climbed upward he also noticed that the path was much more rugged than before, for rocks and stones had fallen down upon it from above, making it almost impassable in certain places. As no obstacle could stop this involuntary traveller, he went on over rolling stones and jagged rocks, and nearing the top of the pass discovered that every trace of vegetation had vanished, and that the place formerly so fertile was now covered with barren rocks and vast fields of snow. Raising his eyes to the peaks all around him he perceived that oaks, beeches, and pines had all vanished, and that the steep mountain sides were heavily coated with ice, which ran far down into the valleys in great frozen streams.

The sight of all this desolation, which had taken the place of such luxuriant vegetation, proved too much for poor Ahasuerus, who sank down on a rock by the wayside and burst into tears. There he sat and sobbed, as he realised for the first time the blighting effect of his passage. His tears flowed so freely that they trickled down into a rocky basin, and when he rose to pursue his way down into the Hasli valley, he left a little lake behind him.

In spite of the masses of snow and ice all

around, and of the cold winds which constantly sweep over that region, the waters of the lake still remain as warm as the tears which fell from Ahasuerus's eyes; and no fish are ever found in this pool.

Still, notwithstanding the desolate landscape, Ahasuerus found the spirit of hospitality not quite dead, for far up on the pass rose a shelter for weary travellers, where they were carefully tended by pious monks. But even here he could not rest, and as he passed along down the mountain, he heard the thunder of falling avalanches behind him. It is during this last journey that he is supposed to have lost the queer old shoe which was long treasured in one of the vaults of the Bern Library.

It is also said that when pausing at one of the huts in the Hasli valley, he sorrowfully foretold that when fate brought him there for the fourth and last time, the whole fruitful valley, from the top of the mountains down to the Lake of Brienz, would be transformed into a huge unbroken field of ice, where he would wander alone in quest of the final resting-place which until now has been denied him, although Eugene Field claims he found it in the New World.[1]

---

[1] See " The Holy Cross," by Eugene Field.

This account of the passage of the Wandering Jew is told with slight variations of all the passes between Switzerland and Italy. Every particularly barren spot in the former country is supposed to have been blighted because he passed through there, or because mortals sinned so grievously that they brought a curse down upon it.

ALTHOUGH travellers coming over the Grimsel often make their way from there to Grindelwald, in the heart of the Oberland, this point is most easily reached from Interlaken, by means of the railroad following the course of an Alpine stream, the Lütchine, which flows in a rocky bed between tall cliffs and steep pine-clad hills. After passing Burglauenen, of which the same story is told as of Roll on the Lake of Thun, you come to Grindelwald, where you have the best view of the Wetterhorn.

A picturesque legend claims that in the Golden Age, when no snow or ice had ever been seen in Switzerland, rich pastures lay between the Faulhorn and the Siedelhorn. A fine brook flowing through there supplied the cattle with all the water they needed, and enabled the herdsmen to keep all their pails and pans in a state of dazzling whiteness and immaculate purity. The pasture was so rich, and the cows gave such quantities of milk, that the men were always tired of milking long before they were through. Spoiled by too great plenty, and over-inclined to take their ease, these men cursed cows and pasture, so a great change soon took place, which at first struck them as very welcome, because as the kine's milk decreased their work diminished.

But one day a maiden came to Gidi, the principal herdsman, and breathlessly announced that a very strange thing had happened, for the brook was all covered with a very thin sheet of glass! When Gidi heard this, he cried, —

"Then it is high time we should change our pasture!"

He therefore immediately drove his herd down into the valley, where, clearing away the dense forest, he built the little village Gidisdorf, which still bears his name. Since then, that place — more generally known as Grindelwald — has become a great resort for tourists, who are attracted thither by the healthful situation, and by the marvellous views obtainable on all sides. From this place many interesting excursions are possible, among others that to the Scheidegg.

GRINDELWALD.

It seems that the possession of the Great or Hasli Scheidegg was once the cause of a serious dispute between the people of Hasli and Grindelwald. As the matter could not be settled otherwise, it was to be decided by oath. The people of Grindelwald, who could not swear truthfully that it belonged to them, nevertheless won it by stratagem, for their champion, filling his shoes with earth from his garden at Grindelwald, boldly presented himself before the judge on the disputed land. There he swore in a tone of such intense conviction that he stood upon Grindelwald soil, that the judge, persuaded of the rectitude of his claim, awarded the disputed land to his community.

The perjurer was, however, duly punished for this crime, for even now his soul can find no rest. Mounted the wrong way round upon a ghostly steed, he rides every night from the spot where he committed perjury down to Meiringen; and if one listens attentively one can often hear his sighs and groans as he takes this nightly jaunt.

On either side of the Upper Grindelwald Glacier tower the Wetterhorn and the two Schreckhorn peaks. The latter mountains are said to be haunted by an unhappy chamois-hunter, who insisted on going in pursuit of game, although a terrible storm was raging and his wife frantically implored him to stay at home.

After climbing far up among the rocks, he detected a fine chamois, and crouching near the edge of a fearful abyss, took careful aim and fired. But just then his gun recoiled, and losing his insecure footing, he slipped over the edge. Instead of falling all the way down, however, the hunter landed on a narrow ledge of rock, whence he could not stir, for the cliff rose straight above and fell sheer below him hundreds of feet.

The poor man, unable to move, remained almost in the same position for three days and two nights, when, seeing no hope of escape, and unable to endure his sufferings any longer, he resolved to commit suicide. Writing the story of the accident which had befallen him and of his fatal resolve, he threw the scrap of paper down into the abyss at his feet. Then, reloading his gun, which he had held fast in his fall, he sent an unerring bullet straight through his brain.

Months later the paper was found close by his shattered corpse ; and since then, whenever a storm rages, one can hear the sudden report of a gun, a crashing fall, prolonged heartrending groans, and the people declare it is the suicide repeating the awful tragedy which ended his life.

It seems that there was once a convent at Interlaken where the nuns, unmindful of their vows, led anything but pure lives. Banished after death to the Schreckhorn, these nuns lie buried deep in the snow; but the spots where they rest glitter in a peculiar way, and are known as Snow Eyes. People say that they are placed there to serve as a constant warning to the valley maidens not to follow the example of those dissolute nuns.

A legend claims that St. Martin once came to Grindelwald, and finding a valley too narrow to admit as much sunshine as he deemed necessary for the good of the people, determined to widen it. He therefore resolutely braced his back against the Mettenberg, and jamming his stick hard against the Eiger, pushed with such force that he partly accomplished his purpose. Such was the effort he made, that the imprint of his back can still be seen in the Mettenberg and a final thrust of his staff punched a hole through the Eiger! This perforation, far up the mountain, is known as the Heiterloch or Martinsloch, and the sun always shines through it on St. Martin's Day, to keep bright the memory of the saint who made it.

FAR up on the southwestern side of the Jungfrau, or Virgin Mountain, is a desolate, icy place, known as the Rothenthal, or Red Valley. In olden times this was one of the most fertile pastures that had ever been seen. And as it was all gemmed over with delicate Alpine flowers, it was generally known as the Alp of the Little Flowers, or the Blümelis Alp.

A beautiful winding road leading right through this valley formed a convenient pass between the cantons of Bern and Valais, and the people there would have been perfectly happy had they not been subject to tyrannical lords. These noblemen were grasping and unprincipled, as well as cruel, and built a castle near the highway so that they could conveniently despoil all travellers and levy supplies from the peasants in the neighbourhood. Not content with these depredations, they cultivated every vice they could think of, and often kidnapped the maidens who happened to please their taste or catch their lustful eyes.

A beautiful and innocent maiden was once tending her cows upon the fragrant Blümelis Alp when the lord of Rothenthal suddenly per-

THE JUNGFRAU.

ceived her, and inflamed by passion suddenly tried to seize her. The poor girl uttered a wild shriek of terror, and looked around her for help. No one was in sight, however, and she already deemed herself lost, when a big black goat suddenly appeared, and rushing against her assailant with lowered horns, bucked him repeatedly, and finally hurled him over the edge of the precipice. The maiden, who had fled when the nobleman let go of her to defend himself against his horned antagonist, turned around just in time to see her persecutor fall. At the same moment the mountains shook violently, and huge masses of ice and rock came crashing down upon the blooming pasture, which, in the twinkling of an eye, was converted into the icy waste you can see there to-day.

Although now seldom trodden by human feet, the Rothenthal is still said to be haunted by the spirits of all those who have oppressed their fellow-men. Here they wander, up and down, bewailing their fate with sighs and groans which can be heard far and wide. Whenever the demons bring a new spirit thither to share their punishment, there is a grand commotion in the Rothenthal,—stones roll, avalanches fall, and the cries and groans become so loud and sustained that the people in the neighbouring valleys, awakening with a start, hide their heads under their blankets and murmur, —

"They are bringing another lord to the Valley!"

A moment later a sudden and stronger gust of wind sweeps past their dwellings; and when it is over, they timidly emerge from their coverings, making the sign of the cross to ward off evil, or softly breathing a prayer to be preserved from harm.

INTERLAKEN is also the usual point of departure for those who wish to visit the valley of Lauterbrunnen, the famous Falls of the Staubbach, and the pastures of Mürren, whence such a beautiful view of the Alps can be obtained, and whence the sunset effects on the glaciers are particularly grand.   As Mr. Samuel Longfellow says, —

> "From Mürren's pastures zoned with snow
>   I watch the peaks, with quickened breath,
>   Flush in the sunset's passionate glow —
>   Fade into pallor passing death." [1]

We are informed that in olden times, before the stream here had hollowed out its deep

____

[1] Poems of Places — Switzerland: Longfellow.

ravine, a herdsman used to exchange long conversations with his beloved, who tended her cattle on the opposite side of the Sausbach. One day when there was a great freshet, and the noise of the roaring waters drowned their voices, the young people, in a playful mood, began to fling handfuls of grass and sod at each other, laughing merrily and making mocking signs whenever one of the harmless missiles reached its goal. In the excitement of the game, however, the young man finally tore up a great lump of loose earth, and unconscious of the fact that a sharp stone lay imbedded deep in it, hurled it with accurate aim straight at the head of his sweetheart. Instead of the half-laughing, half-indignant outcry he fully expected, he suddenly saw the maiden sink lifeless to the ground, for the sharp stone had run straight into her temple !

The broken-hearted youth gave up his herd, withdrew from the company of his former associates, and building a hut on the very spot where the girl he loved had perished, spent the rest of his life in penance and prayer. It is also said that he finally died there, without having known another happy moment, and without ever smiling again.

LEGENDS OF SOLEURE

SOLEURE, on the Aare, in the canton of the same name, is said to be, after Trèves, the oldest city north of the Alps. Most of the old landmarks and fortifications of this city have had to make way for modern improvements ; so the most interesting legends of the region are connected with the pretty drives just outside the city.

In olden times, the picturesque Verenathal, or Verena valley, is said to have been the retreat of a woman so very good and pious that she was known as St. Verena long before her death. This worthy creature, wishing to devote all her time to the worship of God, had betaken herself to this lonely spot, where she built a small hermitage and erected a cross, at the foot of which she spent many hours in fervent prayer. Such was her charity, that she constantly interceded for the wicked, pleading particularly for those who were most likely to succumb to temptation and thus fall into the devil's clutches.

These prayers and intercessions were not without avail ; and the Evil One, perceiving that he could not bag as many souls as usual in that vicinity, finally set out to discover what was the matter. Walking past the hermitage, the sound of passionate and persistent prayer fell upon his ear ; so he noiselessly drew near to ascertain the exact nature of the petition.

Listening attentively, he soon distinguished the words, and gnashed his teeth with rage when he overheard her interceding with special fervour in behalf of the very souls he hoped soon to have in his power. This, then, was the reason for the alarming and otherwise unaccountable decrease in the number of his victims! He therefore resolved that the prayers of the holy woman should immediately be stopped, and with that end in view tore a huge mass of stone from a neighbouring cliff. Then stealing near the saint, he held it for a moment suspended directly above her head, carefully measuring the distance, so that he could kill her with one blow.

But just as he was about to let the mass fall upon Verena and crush her to death, she suddenly looked up, and met his baleful glance with such a look of mingled purity, compassion, and reproach, that Satan, starting back involuntarily, let the rock slip from his nerveless hand. The boulder, falling on his foot, crushed it so badly that he immediately vanished with a wrathful howl of pain and disappointment.

The rock thus dropped by the Evil One can now be seen on the very spot where it fell, and it still bears the distinct imprint of the Devil's claws, which seem burnt in the stone.

> " Wilt thou not believe my legend,
>   Go to St. Verena's glen ;
>   In the rocky clump thou 'lt see there
>   Print of Satan's fingers ten." [1]

Since then, his Infernal Majesty is said to have systematically avoided passing through the narrow gorge where he met with this unpleasant accident.   But he is constantly reminded of St. Verena and of his luckless attempt, for his crushed foot never recovered from this accident, and he has walked lame from that day to this.

Near the hermitage hallowed by the holy life and death of St. Verena, there is a tiny chapel ; and a little farther on one can see a representation of the Holy Sepulchre, hewn out of the rock, and adorned with life-size statues.   This place is frequently visited by pilgrims, who also stand in awe and wonder before the fountains of the

---

[1] Poems of Places — Switzerland: Longfellow.

Soleure Cathedral, which represent Moses striking the rock, and Gideon wringing the dew out of the fleece, which, by a miracle, was dripping wet when all the ground around it was dry.

NOTED as a railway junction, as well as a pleasantly located town on the Aare, Olten is only five miles distant from the pretty health resort of Frohburg, on the Hauenstein. From this eminence one can enjoy a wonderful panorama of the Alps, extending from the Sentis at the extreme northwest, to Mont Blanc at the southeastern end of the mighty range of snow-capped mountains.

Within a few minutes' walk from the hotel of Frohburg, are the ruins of a castle of the same name. once famous for its beauty as well as its great strength. The owner of this castle, the last Count of Frohburg, was known far and wide as a wealthy and powerful nobleman, who ruled his people with a heavy hand. His lands, extending for miles around the castle, were carefully parcelled out among the peasants, who, beside the feudal service required of them by their exacting master, were further compelled to give him one tenth of all the produce of their little farms.

On the day appointed for the payment of the

grain tithes, the lord of Frohburg, standing on the battlements of his castle, yearly beheld the approach of a train of wheat-laden wagons, which formed an unbroken line several miles long. Indeed, it is said that when the first cart vanished under the tunnel-like gateway of the castle, the last could just be seen crossing the bridge at Olten, more than five miles away.

All this wealth and power, however, only tended to spoil the Count of Frohburg, who daily grew more haughty and overbearing, and finally persuaded himself that his vassals had been created for his good pleasure only, and were not human beings like himself. This belief made him extremely cruel and tyrannical, but his overweening pride was soon to be severely punished.

One day, shortly after the grain tithes had been paid, while the lord of Frohburg was away from home, a terrible earthquake suddenly shook the whole range of the Jura Mountains. The castle of Frohburg, unable to withstand the awful shock, although its owner proudly averred it would stand forever, was soon reduced to a heap of unsightly ruins, from which rose dense clouds of choking dust. Towers and battlements, halls and dungeons, were all laid low, and a messenger set off in great haste to apprise the Count of the utter destruction of his abode.

This emissary met his master on the bridge, where he breathlessly and tremblingly imparted his bad tidings. No sooner had the Count heard his report, than he flew into an awful passion, cursing and swearing so vehemently that all the people shrank away from him in horror. In his anger at his loss, and further enraged by his retainers' evident reluctance to remain in the company of a blasphemer, the lord of Frohburg raised his right hand to heaven and threateningly cried, —

" As true as I am lord of the land, not one of you shall again till his fields, until my castle has been rebuilt by the work of your hands ! "

At these words the distressed people groaned aloud, for the castle was a huge edifice, and many months of arduous labour would be necessary before it again rose in all its strength and magnificence. Forced to work without pay for their cruel lord, they would be doomed to starve to death with their wives and children, while the fields which had been so productive hitherto would lie fallow and bare.

While they still stood there in speechless dismay, a thunderbolt suddenly fell from a cloudless sky upon the cruel lord of Frohburg, who soon lay before them a blackened and lightning-scarred corpse. Thus, in the midst of his vassals, Providence punished the wicked man for his cruelty and blasphemy.

As this nobleman was the last of his race, the Castle of Frohburg was never rebuilt. It can still be seen, a mass of ruins, as it was left by the memorable earthquake of 1356, which made such a havoc among the buildings in the Jura mountains.

THE SPALENTHOR (OR THE SPALEN GATE)
BASEL.

BASEL

BASEL, the capital of the canton of the same name, was founded by the Romans before Christ. After serving as one of their military posts, it became a free town under the empire, and at the very beginning of the sixteenth century joined the Swiss Confederation.

The centre of a bishopric founded by Charlemagne, this city was already famous in his day for its churches, monasteries, and schools, although the present cathedral was built only two hundred years later. It suffered sorely from the great earthquake of 1356, when tradition asserts that the building rocked so portentously that a huge bell of pure silver was hurled from its spire straight into the Rhine. There it still lies, and on clear days can be seen shining deep down under the water. Sometimes, too, its sound can be heard there, for the Rhine spirits — who are all good Christians — ring it regularly at the appointed hours for prayer.

The old fortifications of the town have nearly all vanished, but the fourteenth-century Spalenthor still stands. Between that gate and the Spalenberg, the Spalen, a ghostly creature, is said to rush every stormy night. None of the inhabitants can describe it exactly, for they have only caught fleeting glimpses of it, although they have frequently heard it pass.

This ghost is variously designated as a sea-horse, a pig, a dragon, or a griffin, but if any one attempts to ascertain its exact nature, by look-ing out of the window when the sound of its flying footsteps is heard, he is duly punished by waking up on the morrow with a very swol-len face. A bold spirit, who once recklessly thrust his head far out of the window to satisfy his curiosity, is said to have been stricken with such sudden and exaggerated inflammation that the window frame had to be removed before he could again draw in his head !

The two divisions of the town, on either side of the river, were long at feud, and this divi-sion was commemorated by a statue on the old bridge, which by means of a curious mechanism continually stuck out a derisive tongue at the people on the other side. This image, locally known as the " Lällenkönig " is now in the city museum. In reply to this insult the people of the opposite side are said to have set up a rival statue, which turned its back in the most contemptuous way to the famous Lällen-könig.[1]

NOT far from the Summer Casino stands the St. Jacob monument, commemorating a battle of the same name fought in 1444. Tradition declares that thirty days before this fight, the people of Basel were warned of its approach by sudden noises high up in the air above them. First came a rush, as of mailed steeds; then a clash like that of contending armies, followed by a din of cries and groans. Although nothing was visible, the people knew full well that Satan's ghostly train was already fighting in the air above them in anticipation of the coming carnage.

When the fight at St. Jacob really took place, Burkard of Landskron — whose ruined castle stands near Basel — sided with the French. He fought all day with such fury that when evening came and the battle was ended, he and his milk-white battle steed were all covered with blood. Gazing around him, Burkard saw the ground strewn with corpses, the grass and bushes drenched with blood, while the very brook ran red with gore.

The warrior, who delighted in warfare, gazed

[1] For this and other legends of Basel, see the author's " Legends of the Rhine."

enraptured at this awful scene; then, patting his horse, he joyfully cried, —

" Ah, old fellow! you and I are bathing in roses to-day, are we not?"

These unfeeling words, which were answered by a gentle neigh from the weary steed, fell upon the dying ears of a brave Swiss, who had gone into battle echoing his companions' dauntless cry. "Our souls to God, our bodies to the enemy!"

Raising himself feebly, he fixed dim, resentful eyes upon the cruel victor; then, recognising in him a bitter foe of his country, his heart swelled once more in violent anger. Too weak to rise and strike another blow with the sword which had done such good service that day, the Swiss fumbled around for a moment, then, seizing a stone dyed red with patriot blood, hurled it straight at Landskron, saying, —

" There, eat one of your roses, you fiend!"

The stone, flung with unerring aim, struck the warrior in the middle of his forehead, and he fell with a crash to the ground, bathed in his own life-blood. This last effort, however, entirely exhausted the patriot, who, after seeing his enemy fall, sank back on the blood-stained sward, where he breathed his last sigh.

The bravery of the small Swiss force which

held out here, hour after hour, against an army twenty or thirty times greater, so surprised Louis XI. that he gladly made peace with the Swiss, who still consider this battle their Thermopylæ.

Not far from the ruined castle of Landskron, and near the village of Ettingen on one of the spurs of the Jura mountains, are the remains of the old castle of Fürstenstein, the home of a lord of Rothberg in the fourteenth century.

A thoroughly virtuous knight, this nobleman married a good wife, and both were equally devoted to their only child, a charming little girl of about four years of age. One day the mother took the little maiden out into the forest, where she let her run about to fill her basket with wood-flowers, and with the tiny wild strawberries whose perfume and flavour are so delicious. The mother sat down in the shade of a big tree, where the little one came every few moments to exhibit some new treasure ; but the Lady of Rothberg sprang to her feet in terror when a sharp cry rang suddenly through the air.

Rushing to the place where her child had stood a moment before, she now beheld a frightfully steep precipice, but when she leaned far over the edge, frantically calling the child, nothing but a loud echo replied.

Beside herself with grief, the unhappy mother rushed down the mountain path, wildly imploring the Virgin to protect her babe. On reaching the foot of the mountain, and the entrance to the ravine, she almost fainted with joy, for her little girl came running joyfully forward to meet her. The mother clasped the child rapturously to her breast, and when the first emotion was over, and she had assured herself that her darling was uninjured, she gently began to question her. The little maiden artlessly related that she had gone very near the edge of the precipice to pick a beautiful flower, and had suddenly fallen. But before she could touch the ground, she was caught in the arms of a beautiful woman, who gently set her down upon the soft grass, pointing out the red strawberries which grew there in profusion and which she had begun to pick for her father.

This miraculous rescue of their only child filled the parents' hearts with such gratitude that they built a rock chapel on the spot where the little one fell. An image of the Virgin was placed in this building, which soon became a resort for pilgrims coming from far and from near to pray at the shrine of Maria im Stein. Later on, a

Benedictine abbey, Mariastein, was erected near here ; and a fine church now rises on the crag just above the rock-hewn commemorative chapel.

THE ruined castle of Waldenburg, near the village of the same name, was once the home of an exacting nobleman, who required such hard and continual labour from his numerous vassals, that they had no time to till the fields destined to supply their families with food.

One poor man had been kept so persistently at work for his lord, that his wife and children were in sore need. When a messenger came to require further service, he desperately seized a dish, and holding it out to him, declared he would work no more, unless that vessel were filled thrice a day with wholesome food for his starving family.

When the messenger gave this answer to the cruel lord, the latter immediately clapped the recalcitrant vassal into a damp prison, vowing he should remain there until he died miserably among the toads and other vermin which infested it.

The poor wife, driven almost frantic by the cries of her hungry children, painfully wended her way up to the castle one cold winter day, and meeting her master as he rode out of the gate on his way to the chase, fell on her knees in front of him, begging for her husband's release.

The lord of Waldenburg, who did not even know the meaning of the word compassion, roughly bade her rise, threatening to trample her under foot like the rest of the dirt if she did not immediately get out of his way. But the woman still knelt on, pleading for her husband and for the hungry children who had no bread.

Motioning to his huntsman to give her one of the stones by the wayside, the lord now mockingly cried, —

"There is bread for your children. It will last all the longer because it is so hard; but when they have eaten it, you may come again, and I will give you some more of the same kind."

This unfeeling remark proved too much for the outraged mother and wife. She sprang indignantly to her feet and cursed her master with trembling lips, saying that she wished his whole body might be turned into stone as hard and cold as his heart.

At that instant, the lord of Waldenburg felt a strange chill run through his veins, his muscles suddenly stiffened, and before he could move

or even utter a sound, he and his steed were
petrified. His vassals, seeing Heaven had
avenged them, now rushed into the castle, freed
the prisoners, took possession of all the money
and food, and in passing out again taunted the
stone image of the man who had wronged them
so persistently.

This stone knight still mounts solemn guard
near the entrance of his former castle, although
wind and weather have so disintegrated the
once hard rock that its primitive shape is now
almost unrecognisable.

In many parts of Switzerland, the noisy June
bugs are known as thunder bugs. Near Basel,
as well as at Ormond, the following amusing
story is told of some simple peasants who dwelt
in a deep valley. A long drought had made
the soil so hard and dry that the people feared
their harvests would be ruined unless they soon
had rain. As their prayers and processions
proved alike unavailing, they longed to try
some more efficacious means of rain-making.

A joker, hearing their quandary, now gravely
bade them go to Basel and buy a little thunder
at the drug-store there, assuring them that if
they only let it loose in their valley, the rain
would soon follow. The peasants, hearing this,

immediately sent a deputation to the city, and entering the largest and most fashionable apothecary shop, the rustic spokesman confidentially informed the clerk that he had come to buy some thunder.

The clerk, who was not devoid of humour, gravely asked a few leading questions, then went into the rear of the store, saying he would get what they wanted. Stepping out into the garden unseen, he caught a few June bugs, and packed them carefully in a large pill-box. This he wrapped up and solemnly delivered to the waiting peasants, making such a very small charge that they openly regretted not having known sooner that thunder could be purchased so cheap in Basel.

The men now set out on their return journey to the Frickthal, and as the apothecary had gravely charged them not to open the box until they reached their village, they passed the little parcel from hand to hand, weighed and shook it, and grinned at each other with delight when they heard a faint rumbling noise within it.

Their impatience to see what this thunder might look like so engaged their attention that they did not notice dark clouds looming up behind them, and when they reached the top of the mountain at the foot of which lay their village, they determined to wait no longer and opened the box. With a loud buzz and a bang, the June bugs, resenting their imprisonment and violent shaking, now flew, as luck would have it, directly over the village, while the deputation raced wildly down the mountain side with empty pill-box !

The people were all on the market-place ready to receive them, and as soon as they appeared, clamoured to see the thunder they had purchased. The men sheepishly confessed what they had done, but declared all would yet be right, because the thunder bugs had flown straight over the village, and the rain would doubtless soon follow. Fortunately for them, the first black cloud just then appeared over the top of the mountain, and the people, perceiving it, gave a loud shout of joy. In an almost incredibly short space of time, all the Frickthalers were obliged to take refuge in their dwellings, for the rain came down in torrents, drenching the soil which had been so parched, and thus saving all the people from the threatened famine.

AARGAU

IN early days when men were simple-minded
and pious, two lovely children were often
seen hovering over the Aargau grain fields when
the ears were just beginning to form. A boy
and a girl, with golden curls waving over plump
white shoulders, and gleaming white garments
flowing down to the tiny feet which barely
touched the swaying grain, this little pair flitted
on from field to field, with dimpled hands out-
stretched as if in blessing.

Wherever they passed a golden gleam rested
like a halo upon the land, where they were generally known as the Grain Angels, and people
knew that a fine harvest was assured. These
radiant little cherubs were the spirits of two
little children, who, straying into a harvest
field, lost their way and died there like the
fabled Babes in the Woods.

THE people of Brugg once agreed to assemble
on the next rainy day, and sallying forth in a
body, plant an extensive oak forest near their

quaint little city. As soon as the sky darkened, therefore, and the rain began to fall, they all went out, thrust sharp sticks into the damp ground, dropped acorns into the holes thus made, and pushing the dirt down with their feet, pressed it down hard. As men, women, and children took part in this sowing-bee, twelve acres were soon planted, and when the wet workers came back to town, the magistrates rewarded them by giving each a small wheaten roll.

The acorns thus consigned to the soil failed to grow because planted too deep. so the expedition was repeated on the following year, the seed being now laid in furrows instead of separate holes. This system of planting proving equally unsuccessful, the Brugg magistrates, on the third year, bade the inhabitants go forth into a neighbouring forest, dig up promising young trees, and plant them carefully on the spot where the future forest was to stand.

This third attempt, made in 1532, was turned into a sort of picnic by the merry children, who, singing in chorus, carried the young oaks to the appointed place, where each carefully planted the chosen tree. When they came home, the magistrates again gave each child a roll, and invited the older people to a grand public banquet where all drank to the success of the young oaks.

This time the trees throve apace, and on every anniversary of this famous oak-planting, the little ones march in gay procession all around the woods and come home brandishing green branches, to prove to their parents that the forest is doing well. This quaint procession of wands, or Ruthenzug, has been kept up for centuries, and we are told the Brugg school-children enjoy it to-day as much as any of their ancestors.

THE mineral springs at Baden were once under the protection of three wise women, who, although no one knew who they were or whence they came, were generally supposed to have inhabited the old castle of Stein.

Although usually on duty near the springs, these wise dames avoided being seen by the bathers, but if the water were defiled in any way, or if any of the rules were disregarded, they suddenly and mysteriously checked the flow of the healing waters, and did not allow another drop to run until the impurities were removed, or the wrong-doing ceased.

The wise women of Baden were particularly

careful of the Verena spring, so called because
the saint of that name once bathed in its waters.
Into that basin they directed a stream of mineral
waters of special potency when used by women
and children. Sick babies plunged into this
healing flood emerged rosy and well, and the
women who came here to recover lost health
or to secure the blessing of offspring, were
sure soon to see the fulfilment of their dearest
hopes.

The three guardian spirits of the Baden
springs were so beautiful and benevolent that
the people likened them to the Virgin, and at a
loss for another appellation designated them the
three Marys. Their memory is not only treasured at Baden, but it is also enshrined in a
nursery rhyme, to which all German-speaking
children are trotted in Switzerland.

> " Rite, rite Rössli,
> Ze Bade stoht e Schlössli,
> Ze Bade stoht e güldi Hus,
> Es lueged drei Mareie drus.
> Die eine spinnt Side,
> Die andere schnützelt Chride,
> Die dritt schnit Haberstrau,
> B'hüet mir Gott das Chindle au ! "

AT Wettingen, the building now occupied by
the Normal School was once an old abbey

founded in 1227 by Henry, Count of Rapperswyl. This nobleman was so good and pious that he spent most of his time in pilgrimages, thereby winning the nickname of The Wanderer. Returning from the Holy Land, he once found himself in imminent danger of perishing in the waves, and fixing his eyes upon a bright star which suddenly shone through a break in the stormy sky, he made a solemn vow to build a monastery at Wettingen should his life be spared.

This prayer was evidently heard, for the storm soon abated and the ship came safely to land. When the Count of Rapperswyl therefore reached home, he founded the abbey, which, in memory of his vow, and of the star he saw at sea, was called Maria Stella, or Meer Stern, the Star of the Sea.

The handsome old castle of Hallwyl, the ancestral home of a noble Swiss family of the same name, stands on the road between Lucerne and Lenzburg, near the Lake of Hallwyl.

A lord of Hallwyl had three sons, and as the two elder ones died early, the third had to drop his clerical studies and prepare to fulfil his duties as future head of his house. Although this young man duly married and had a fine son, it seems that he never ceased to regret his interrupted priestly career, but, surrounded by monks of all kinds, spent his time in religious practices and in poring over homilies and church records.

None too strong to begin with, these long vigils and fasts so undermined his health, that he finally became dangerously ill. One day, fearing that he was about to die, he vowed he would send his son on a pilgrimage to the Holy Land should he recover. True to this promise, the lord of Hallwyl no sooner left his bed than he recalled his son, who was fighting under Rudolf of Hapsburg, and bade him set out immediately for the Holy Sepulchre. The young man, who thought his services more needed at home, nevertheless prepared to obey, for a vow was a sacred matter and children in those days rarely ventured to question parental orders.

At parting the old lord of Hailwyl broke his ring in two, telling the young man that when death overtook him he would leave his half to his father confessor. The latter would administer the estates carefully, giving them up to none but the man who established his right to them by producing the other half of the broken ring.

It took twenty years for John of Hallwyl to fulfil his father's vow. During that time the old man died, and the monks took possession of castle and estates. They were so determined not to give them up again, however, that they not only announced the death of young Hallwyl, but turned out of his castle an orphaned relative to whom he had been betrothed in her infancy according to his mother's wish. Alone and friendless, — for she refused to yield to the monks' suggestions and enter a convent,— this young girl would have died of want, had not the lord of Müllinen, a friend of her betrothed, offered her a home with his mother and sister in his own castle.

Clémence gratefully accepted this kind proposal, and as she had been a mere babe when John of Hallwyl started out on his perilous journey, she did not prove faithless to him when she unconsciously fell in love with his noble friend.

Now it happened that John of Hallwyl was not dead, as many supposed. On the contrary, he was even then on his way home to claim his estates. The monks, hearing this by accident, and determined to keep his property, hired highwaymen to lie in wait for him and murder him before he could reach Hallwyl and make himself known. This bold plan might have succeeded, had not the lord of Müllinen

chanced to hunt near the place where the highwaymen were ambushed. Hearing the noise of
a fight, he spurred rapidly forward, and perceiving a knight on the point of succumbing to
a large force, made such a gallant charge that
the robbers fled.

When Müllinen bent over the prostrate form
of the man he had rescued, he found him grievously wounded, and had him carefully carried
home. There, when the traces of blood had
been gently removed, he recognised in the
stranger his long-absent friend. Of course, he
and the ladies now vied with each other in caring for Hallwyl, who, becoming aware during
his convalescence of the affection existing between his friend and betrothed, generously
released her and bade them be happy together.

As soon as he was sufficiently recovered he
presented himself before the monks to claim
his inheritance. They, however, pretended not
to recognise him, but politely declared that if
he could produce a fragment of ring exactly fitting the one entrusted to their keeping by the
last lord of Hallwyl, they would gladly surrender the castle to him.

Hearing this, John of Hallwyl immediately
presented the broken ring, and the monks sent
for the casket in which they preserved the

token left by the deceased. To John's surprise
and indignation, however, it failed to fit his half
of the circlet, and the monks called him an
impostor and dismissed him empty-handed.

Hallwyl and his friend now rode back to
Müllinen, determined to appeal to the feudal
court of Aargau for justice. There, both parties
were called upon to expose their case and take
their oath, but as the judge was entirely at a
loss to decide which was right, he decreed the
matter should be settled by a judiciary duel between John of Hallwyl and a champion selected
by the monks.

On the appointed day, and in the presence of
all the lords and ladies of the country, Hallwyl
met his opponent in the lists, and after a fearful struggle and the display of almost fabulous
strength and courage succeeded in defeating
him. Then, while the monks' champion lay
where he had fallen, slowly dying from his
many wounds, he suddenly confessed aloud that
he and a band of assassins had been hired to
waylay and kill Hallwyl on his return home.

Before he could add another word he expired,
but the monks one and all solemnly declared
that the poor man was raving, for they had
always been willing to relinquish possession of
the Hallwyl estates to any one who produced

the right token. The mendacity of this statement was soon proved, however, for a dying
jeweller confessed that he had been hired to
make an exact copy of the broken ring, but
altering its shape in such a way that the fragment in the young man's possession would fail
to fit it.

John of Hallwyl, having thus recovered his
estates, soon went off to war again, and only
when weary of fighting came home, married,
and brought up several sons whose descendants
still live in different parts of the country to-day.

The ring of Hallwyl is noted in Swiss art and
literature, and the above story forms the theme
of poems, paintings, and historical romances,
which, bearing an unmistakable mediæval imprint, have a peculiar and enduring charm of
their own.

At the foot of the Wülpelsberg, on the right
of the beautiful Aare valley, are the Schinznach
sulphur baths, so frequently visited by French
and Swiss sufferers from skin diseases.

One of the favourite walks from this point
leads up the mountain to the ruins of Hapsburg
Castle, the most famous of all Swiss strong-
holds. Founded in 1020, it is the cradle of the
imperial family of Austria, in whose hands it

remained for more than two centuries. Then, by papal decree, it passed out of their keeping, and was Swiss property until the Canton of Aargau presented it as a wedding gift to Rudolf, the prince imperial, on his marriage with a Belgian princess. Only one crumbling tower of the famous castle now stands, but the ruins are surrounded by such a halo of history, legend, and romance, that they are particularly attractive to all visitors.

The founders of this castle, the Counts of Altenburg, trace their genealogy back to the seventh century, when their ancestors ruled in Alsacia and Alemannia. Rich and influential even at this early date, these noblemen sought to extend their possessions by every means in their power. Their repeated encroachments upon their neighbours' dominions were not accepted without protest, however, and when the emperor, in answer to frantic appeals for justice, bade them relinquish the territory to which they could lay no rightful claim, they assumed so defiant an attitude that an armed struggle soon ensued. The upshot of this conflict was that the grasping noblemen were despoiled of the main part of their estates, forced to leave Alsacia, and they took refuge in Helvetia, where they had already acquired some property. There they built new homes at Wohlen, Altenburg, and Muri, where, by fair means and by foul, they continued their policy of self-aggrandisement until their shattered fortunes were fully restored.

The sun of prosperity shining brightly over their heads once more, these noblemen again openly defied the imperial authority. But, taught by experience, they wisely resolved to prepare for future emergencies by erecting an impregnable fortress, in which they and their dependents could successfully resist even the emperor's forces.

Gazing about them for the most favourable site for their projected stronghold, the Altenburgs finally decided upon the Wülpelsberg. Tradition relates, however, that while they were still hesitating where to build their future castle, Count Radbod of Altenburg went out hawking one day. While he was flying his birds in the Aare valley, one of them got away, and refusing to obey his call, flew off to a neighbouring height. Loath to lose his favourite bird, Count Radbod set out in pursuit of it, scrambled up the wooded slopes of the Wülpelsberg, nor paused until he caught the truant hawk, which was perched on the topmost ridge of the mountain.

The bird duly secured and hooded, Count Radbod — who had been too intent upon its capture to pay any attention to his surroundings — looked about him to find his bearings, and remained spell-bound before the magnificent view he now beheld.

At his feet lay the Birrfeld, — a plain where Constantius Chlorus fought a bloody battle against the Alemans in 303. Many thriving villages now dot this part of the country, and their gables and church spires rise here and there among flourishing fruit trees. But the modern traveller's glance rests by preference upon the peaceful hamlet where Pestalozzi, founder of the kindergarten and prince of educators, spent the last few years of a useful life.

Count Radbod gazed enraptured at the extensive forests, and the picturesque valleys of the Aare, the Limmat, and the Reuss, tracing the course of these mountain streams to the point where they meet and merge into one, near the site of the old Roman station, Vindonissa. Then his eyes rested upon the green hills rising in ever widening circles around him, while above and behind them towered the Alps, like a host of snow-clad angels mounting silent guard over the matchless landscape.

Charmed with the prospect before him, and

quickly perceiving the strategic value of the location, Count Radbod immediately determined to build his fortress on the spot where he had caught his hawk, calling it the Hawk's Castle, or Habichtsburg, in memory of the circumstances under which this decision had been reached.

The castle was therefore duly begun, the walls being built strong and thick so as to resist every attack. Still, only a small part of the funds furnished by the family for the erection of the stronghold was devoted to that purpose, for Radbod wisely used the main portion to acquire numerous friends, vassals, and servants, who promised to stand by him and his in time of danger.

The castle was not entirely finished when Radbod's brother, Bishop Werner, announced his visit to inspect the work. Upon receipt of this news, Count Radbod summoned his dependents, bade them hide in the neighbourhood, and noiselessly surround the fortress at a given signal. Then he went to meet the Bishop and escort him up to the new castle. Werner sincerely admired the location and strength of the building, but found fault because it was not flanked by outer walls and towers, and because the interior was so bare of all ornamentation. He finally asked Radbod somewhat testily what had become of all the money sent him, for it was self-evident it had not all been expended on the fortress.   Radbod good-naturedly bade the bishop cease his grumbling and go to bed, promising to prove on the morrow that every penny had been wisely invested in making the castle impregnable and in strengthening their position in the land.

At sunrise, on the following day, Werner rose from his couch, and going to the window gazed in speechless admiration at the view.   But while he stood there, feasting his eyes upon the flame-tipped glaciers, his attention was suddenly attracted by shadowy forms, which, starting up from behind every rock, shrub, and tree at his feet, stealthily surrounded the castle.   In terror lest the imperial forces — whose coming he always dreaded — should have stolen a march upon him, and lest he and his brother should fall into the enemy's hands, the bishop rushed to the door to give the alarm.   But on the threshold he met Count Radbod, who, smiling at his fright, quietly said, —

" Rest without fear, my brother.   The men you see yonder are your vassals and mine, fully armed for our defence.   I acquired their services with the funds entrusted to my care, for I knew strong walls would prove of little avail, unless defended by stout hearts and willing hands."

This answer, and the sight of the brave men now drawn up in military array for his inspection, more than satisfied the bishop, who, accepting Radbod's invitation, betook himself to the great hall of the castle, where he received the oath of fealty and the respectful homage of the new retainers of his race. Since then, all the members of the old Altenburg family have been known as the counts of Habsburg, or Hapsburg, a modification of the old Habichtsburg.[1]

The Hapsburgs throve apace in their new home, their power increasing until even the freemen of the land humbly besought their protection in exchange for the payment of certain taxes. But the ascendency thus gained by these noblemen made them more arrogant and tyrannical than ever, so that they finally considered themselves owners of the land, and lords of the free people they were gradually exasperating by their arbitrary treatment.

In those days, the greatest of all the Hapsburg race, Rudolf III., was born in the castle, the emperor being his sponsor. At twenty-one, owing to the early death of his father, Rudolf

---

[1] See the author's " Legends of the Rhine."

became head of the family, and began that career of warfare and conquest for which he is noted in history. Afraid of nothing, and ready to grasp at everything, his neighbours soon learned to dread him, and the Bishop of Basel — with whom he had a feud — expressed the general opinion of his congeners by crying out once in comical dismay, —

" Sit firm upon Thy throne, O Lord God, or the Count of Hapsburg will crowd Thee, too, out of it ! "

Still, Rudolf was so frank and genial, that he won many friends and adherents, and his sturdy warriors were particularly devoted to him, because he shared all their fatigues, cheerfully partook of their frugal fare, and was even seen by their camp fire diligently mending his worn garments.

When Rudolf could not compass his ends by force, he frequently resorted to ruse. For instance, wishing to take a castle on the Uetliberg near Zürich, which was owned by a Robber-Knight who despoiled all the citizens passing along that way, he devised the following stratagem. Thirty tall and strong horsemen, mounted upon sturdy steeds, were directed each to take a companion behind him, and ride up the mountain. A force of thirty men had no terrors for

the Robber-Knight, who boldly sallied forth
with his garrison to attack them. But when
he found himself face to face with double that
number, he fled in terror followed by all his
retainers. Rudolf's small force now entered
the wide-open gates of the castle, and after dis-
posing of its occupants and riches, razed it to
the ground.

While administering his affairs in person,
Rudolf proved a kind and just master, and often
sat under the linden-tree at Altorf, to award
justice to the freemen of Uri, who had chosen
him as their umpire. But while he was away,
upholding the tottering fortunes of the Hohen-
stauffens, or extending his domains, his bailiffs
and stewards ruled with a rod of iron over the
estates he had won. Such were their exactions,
that the people of Uri, Schwyz, and Unterwald,
who had long prided themselves upon their independence, finally determined to recover their
freedom. In 1245 they openly rebelled, but
while Uri recovered its lost liberty, and was
again allowed to depend directly from the
crown, Schwyz and Unterwald were compelled
to remain under the overlordship of the Hapsburg race.

THE FOREST CANTONS

RUDOLF VON HAPSBURG'S many possessions included an old castle on the
Ramflue, which, although it is said to have been
founded by the Romans, was known as Neu
Hapsburg. Charmingly located on the banks of
the Lake of Lucerne, this castle was a favourite
resort of Rudolf, who went thither, in the in-
tervals of fighting, to hunt the chamois and the
deer.

Tradition claims that Rudolf once set out for
the chase from Neu Hapsburg, mounted upon
his favourite steed, and followed by one squire,
who rode an inferior horse, and therefore had
some trouble in keeping up with his rapid pace.
While crossing a beautiful green meadow, Rudolf's attention was suddenly attracted by a
tinkling sound. His curiosity aroused, he
spurred ahead in the direction of the noise,
and soon beheld a priest carrying the Sacrament,
and preceded by a sacristan dutifully ringing a
little bell.

At this sight, Rudolf immediately dismounted.
Then, kneeling, he did respectful homage to the

Blessed Body of our Lord, and in that humble posture watched the little procession pass along its way. A few moments later, he sprang up surprised, for the priest had come to a sudden standstill. After a brief period of evident hesitation, Rudolf saw him set the Host down upon a neighbouring stone, and begin to remove his sandals and gird up his cassock. Hastening toward him, Rudolf perceived that recent heavy rains had so swollen the mountain torrent which flowed through the meadow, that the rude bridge had been entirely swept away. No other means of crossing being available for many miles, the priest had determined to wade through the ice-cold waters, for that was his only chance of reaching the dying man who had begged for the last sacrament.

After vainly trying to dissuade the priest from a struggle with the cold and rushing stream, Rudolf, impressed by the good man's devotion to duty, suddenly offered him his steed. The priest demurred at first, but realising he might not reach his parishioner in time if he had to wade through every torrent, he gratefully accepted the offer. Rudolf then helped him mount the fiery steed, and, once safely across the torrent, saw him speed away to the dying man, whom he reached just in time to bestow

the last consolations of religion and thus smooth
his path to the grave.

In the meantime, Rudolf patiently awaited
the coming of his squire, then mounting the
latter's palfrey went on his way. But, early
next morning, the priest appeared at Neu
Hapsburg, leading the borrowed steed by the
bridle, and he warmly expressed his gratitude for
the timely loan of a mount whose strength and
speed had enabled him to reach and comfort a
dying man. When he added, however, that he
had come to restore the animal to its owner,
Rudolf impetuously cried : " God forbid that I,
or any of my men, should ever use again for
war or the chase the steed which bore the
sacred Body and Blood of our Blessed Lord ! "
Then he formally presented the horse to the
priest, to have and to hold for ever, bidding
him use it for the fulfilment of his holy duties.

Later, on that selfsame day, Rudolf visited
a convent, where a nun suddenly addressed him
saying : " My lord, you honoured the Almighty
by the timely gift of your horse. This good
deed will not remain unrewarded, for it has
been revealed to me that you and yours will
attain the highest temporal honors."

The castle of Neu Hapsburg was destroyed
by the inhabitants of Lucerne in 1352, but since

then the peasants have declared that the ruins are haunted by the spirits of departed knights and ladies. A peasant girl, rowing past there early in the morning and late at night, said she often saw a gayly dressed company. Sometimes the knights and ladies made friendly signs to her, but at others the men were all in armour and terrified her by their threatening gestures. Encouraged by their signs, she once stepped ashore to watch them play on the grassy slope with disks of bright gold, which she vainly tried to catch in her apron and carry home.

The nun's prediction to Rudolf was duly fulfilled, for the priest who had received his steed, having become chaplain to the Bishop of Mayence, used his influence to such good purpose that he secured Rudolf's election to the imperial crown of Germany, in 1273. Schiller, in his poem "The Count of Habsburg," claims that at the coronation feast at Aix-la-Chapelle an aged minstrel brought tears to the eyes of all the guests by singing a touching ballad, describing the good deed performed by the new emperor, when he was only a count.

Rudolf proved as successful as ambitious while seated on the German throne, but as the imperial crown was elective and not hereditary, he secured for his descendants Austria,

Styria, and Carinthia. These lands were won during a war with the king of Bohemia, and have ever since formed the patrimony of the Hapsburg race, which has provided many rulers for Europe, America, and India.

When Rudolf died in 1291, the imperial crown was disputed by two candidates, until, by the death of one of them, it finally fell into the hands of Albert of Hapsburg, Rudolf's son. As grasping and tyrannical as any of his race, Albert refused to let his nephew John — the son of an older brother — have the Castle of Hapsburg, which was his by right of inheritance. Embittered by this act of injustice, and despairing of redress since the wrong was committed by the emperor himself, John began to plot with several malcontents, biding his time until he could take his revenge by slaying his uncle.

John was not the only one who complained of injustice. The freemen of Helvetia also had good cause for resentment. On mounting the imperial throne, Rudolf had refused to confirm Uri's charter, and his bailiffs and stewards ruthlessly exerted the power entrusted to them. Thus, they gradually alienated the peaceful peasants, and drove them to the verge of despair. Mindful of their former independence, and weary of tyranny and extortion, the principal citizens of the cantons of Uri, Schwyz, and Unterwald met, seventeen days after Rudolf's death, and on the 1st of August, 1291, took a solemn oath to stand by each other and resist all foreign intervention, until they had recovered their former freedom. This oath — the corner-stone of the Swiss Confederation — was duly sworn by all the principal inhabitants, among which figure men whose names are noted in legend as well as in history.

Tradition has richly supplemented the meagre historical data of this epoch, thus giving us one of the most romantic, if not authentic, chapters of Swiss history. The legend, which gradually arose, has been the theme of Schiller's tragedy of " William Tell," of Rossini's opera of the same name, and a source of inspiration for countless poems, pictures, and statues. Such is the popular belief in the tale, that all the most famous places mentioned in it are always pointed out to strangers, and kept alive in the memory of the public by more or less picturesque monuments.

THE famous Tell legend runs as follows : The stewards and bailiffs of the House of Austria, encouraged by immunity, daily grew more and more cruel, until, under the slightest pretext, they thrust Swiss freemen into damp and dark prisons, keeping them there for life. Fearful stories of the heartlessness of these bailiffs were noised abroad, and no one could speak strongly enough of their greed, cruelty, and total lack of principle.

The Swiss bore this oppression as patiently as they could, and until their position became so unbearable that they perceived they must assert and maintain their rights to freedom, or they would soon be reduced to a state of such abject slavery as to be deprived of all power of resistance. Walter Fürst, Arnold von Melchthal, and Werner Stauffacher, the wealthiest and most respected citizens of the cantons of Uri, Schwyz, and Unterwald, therefore met to discuss the advisability of an uprisal, and, in support of their views, quoted recent acts of wanton cruelty perpetrated by Austrian bailiffs. For instance, one of these men had grievously insulted the wife of a peaceful citizen, who, to defend her, slew the oppressor and was now a hunted fugitive.

A young man of Uri was told he must surrender the fine team of oxen with which he was ploughing, because the bailiff wanted them. As the messenger coolly proceeded to taunt him and unyoke his oxen, the young peasant, in a frantic effort to save the cattle, dealt a blow which raised a terrible outcry among the bailiff's servants. Knowing that such an offence would be punished by life-long imprisonment in some foul dungeon, if not by prolonged torture and cruel death, the young man hastily fled. But the blow so thoughtlessly given was visited upon his aged father, whose eyes were put out by order of the vindictive bailiff.

Countless other examples of fiendish cruelty and wanton oppression were not lacking, and when the three men parted, it was with the understanding that they were to ascertain how many of their countrymen were willing to help them. They furthermore arranged to meet again, October 17, 1307, on the Grütli or Rütli, a plateau at the foot of the Seelisberg, close by the Mythenstein, on the Lake of Lucerne.

One moonlight night, therefore, three bands of ten picked men, led by Fürst, Stauffacher, and Melchthal wended their way to the Grütli, and there beneath the open sky, and in sight of the snow-crowned mountains tipped by the first glow of dawn, the leaders, clasping hands, raised three fingers to heaven. In that position they solemnly swore to shake off the yoke of the oppressor, their motto being, " One for all and all for one." This oath was fervently echoed by the thirty companions they had brought thither, and ere they parted all agreed to be ready to rise at a given signal on New Year's Day, to drive the tyrants out of the land for ever.

On the traditional spot where the Swiss patriots stood while registering this solemn oath, three springs of crystal clear water are said to have sprung. The legend further claims that in one of the clefts of the Seelisberg the patriots sit, wrapped in slumbers which will remain undisturbed until their country again has need of their services.

Swiss peasants say that the Three Tells — for such is their popular designation — have been seen several times. A young shepherd, for instance, seeking a stray goat, once came to the entrance of this mysterious cave, and beheld three men fast asleep. While staring in speechless amazement at their old-fashioned garb and venerable faces, one of the sleepers suddenly awoke and asked, " What time is it up in the world ? "

" High noon," stammered the shepherd, remembering that the sun stood directly overhead when he entered the cave.

" Then it is not yet time for us to appear,"

THE OATH ON THE RÜTLI.

drowsily remarked the aged man, dropping off to sleep again.

The shepherd gazed in silent awe upon the three Tells, then, stealing noiselessly out of the cave, carefully marked the spot, so he could find it again when he wished to return. These precautions were vain, however, for he and his companions searched every nook and cranny in the mountain, without ever being able to find the entrance to the cave of the Swiss Sleepers. But the natives declare that some simple herdsman may again stumble upon it by accident, and many believe that the guardians of their country's liberties will come forth to defend them in case of need.

Among the patriots who took the oath upon the Rütli, was a man named Tell, son-in-law of Walter Fürst, and noted far and wide for his skill as a marksman. Strong and sure-footed, Tell delighted in pursuing the chamois over almost inaccessible heights, and along the jagged edges of dangerous precipices, where a moment's dizziness or a single misstep would have hurled him down on the rocks hundreds of feet below. Tell lived, with his wife and two little sons, in a hut at Bürglen, in Uri, on the very spot where a chapel was built in his honour in 1522.

It came to pass, shortly after the patriots had met on the Grütli, and before the time set for their uprisal, that Gessler, an Austrian bailiff, one of whose castles rose in sight of Hapsburg, determined to ascertain by a clever device how many men in Uri were loyal to his master. He therefore set up a pole in the market-place at Altorf, upon which he hung a hat, — the emblem of Austrian power, — bidding a herald proclaim aloud that all must do homage to it under penalty of death or life-long imprisonment.

The freemen of Uri were justly incensed when they heard this decree, and by common consent avoided passing through the square. When compelled to do so, they resorted to various stratagems to avoid obeying Gessler's orders without forfeiting life or liberty. One of their devices was to send the priest to take up his position with the Host directly under the obnoxious Austrian emblem. Of course, all who now passed by reverently bent the knee ; but it was quite evident, even to the guards, that the homage was paid to the Sacrament alone, and not to the imperial hat.

Living only a short distance from Altorf, but ignorant of all that had recently happened there, Tell came down to the village one day, leading his little son by the hand. Unconscious alike of pole, hat, and guards, he strolled across the square, and was greatly surprised to find himself suddenly arrested for defying Gessler's orders. While protesting his innocence, and striving to make the guards release him, Tell saw Gessler ride by ; so, turning toward him, he loudly called for justice. The bailiff immediately drew near, and standing in the midst of the crowd composed of his attendants and of the startled inhabitants of Altorf, he sneeringly listened to Tell's account of his unjust arrest.

Now, it happened that Gessler had often heard Tell's skill as a marksman loudly praised, and that he had long wished to see an exhibition of it. He therefore seized this opportunity for gratifying both his curiosity and his cruelty, and promised to set the prisoner free, if he shot an apple from the head of his child at a distance of one hundred and fifty paces.

At these words a murmur of indignation arose in the crowd, but such was the fear inspired by the cruel Gessler that none ventured to interfere in behalf of Tell, whose prayers and protestations proved alike vain. Seeing no other means of escape, and urged by his child, who of his own accord ran to place himself against a linden-tree on the spot where the fountain now stands, Tell tremblingly selected two arrows from his quiver. One he hastily thrust in his bosom, the other he carefully adjusted in his crossbow ; but when he would fain have taken aim, the weapon fell from his nerveless hand. Still, a sneer from the bailiff, and an encouraging call from his boy, steeled Tell's heart for this awful test of skill. A moment later the child came bounding forward, proudly exhibiting the apple transfixed by his father's dart.

Just as Tell, still dazed by emotion, was about to turn away, Gessler called him back to inquire why he had drawn two arrows from his quiver, when only one shot was required to prove his proficiency. Tell hesitated ; but when Gessler assured him that he could speak without any fear for his life, he hoarsely answered, —

" Had I injured my child, this arrow would have found its goal in your heart, for my hand would not have trembled a second time ! "

Beside himself with rage at these bold words, Gessler now bade his guards bind Tell fast, and convey him immediately down to his waiting boat at Flühlen, adding that while he would keep his promise not to kill Tell, he would nevertheless thrust him into a dungeon where neither sun nor moon would ever shine upon him, and where snakes would prey upon his living body.

Placed in the boat, with fast-bound hands and

TELL ANSWERS GESSLER.

feet, his useless weapons close beside him, Tell despairingly watched the bailiff embark and the shore near Altorf slowly recede. But when the rowers tried to round the Axenstein, a sudden tempest swept down on the lake, whipping its waters to foam, and bringing skiff and passengers in such imminent danger that there seemed no hope of escape. The boatmen, remembering that Tell was the most clever steersman on the lakeside, now implored Gessler to let him help, and the prisoner, freed from his bonds, quickly seized the rudder.

With strong arm and fearless gaze he stood there, and boldly directed the boat toward a broad ledge of rock forming a natural landing-place at the foot of the Axenberg, at a point where the lake is nearly seven hundred feet deep.

As the boat drew near this place, Tell suddenly let go the rudder, and seizing his bow and arrows, sprang ashore! This spot, since known as Tellsplatte, is one of the most interesting sites on the Lake of Lucerne, and in the chapel commemorating this feat there are several paintings representing various phases of the legend.

Gessler's boat, hurled back among the seething waves, tossed about in great danger, although his boatmen now made frantic efforts to save

their own lives.   Dreading the bailiff's ven-
geance should he manage to escape, Tell hastened over the mountains to the Hohle Gasse,
or Hollow Way, a narrow road between Küss-
nacht and Immensee, along which Gessler would
have to pass to reach home.

There, crouching in the bushes on the steep
bank, Tell patiently waited to see whether his
enemy would escape from the perils of the storm.
Before long the bailiff appeared, riding at the
head of his troop, and evidently meditating in
what way he could best effect his revenge upon
Tell.   His wicked plans were all cut short, however, for an arrow from Tell's bow put a sudden
end to his tyrannical career.   The spot where
Tell stood and where Gessler fell has long been
marked by a small chapel, decorated with a painting representing this scene.   After ascertaining
that Gessler was really dead, Tell fled, making
his way back to Bürglen, where he cheered
friends and family by the assurance that the
tyrant could never trouble them again.

The story of Swiss independence and of Tell's
brave deeds has been so ably dramatised by
Schiller, that a grateful people have carved his
name on the Mythenstein, where it may be
seen by passengers on the boats constantly
plying to and fro on the Lake of Lucerne.

Besides the three picturesque chapels known by the name of Tell, where anniversary services are held every year, and the huge statue erected at Altorf, on the very spot where he shot the apple from the head of his son, Tell's name has been honoured in poetry, painting, sculpture, and song. His death was on a par with the rest of his life, for when far advanced in age, he fearlessly sprang into the Schächen to save a drowning child. The sudden plunge into the ice-cold waters of this mountain stream, and the great exertion required to stem its current, so enfeebled the old man that he soon died.

> " And thus the great life ended;
> God ! — was it not the best
> Of all the deeds of valour
> That won a hero's rest ?
> So mused I by the Schächen ;
> So say we, true and well
> That the last deed was the best deed
> That closed the life of Tell ! "
>
> HENRY MORFORD.[1]

Tradition claims that Gessler's cruel treatment of Tell precipitated historical events, for when the men of Uri, Schwyz, and Unterwald heard that Gessler was dead, they gave the agreed signal for a general uprising. Then they simulta-

---

[1] Poems of Places — Switzerland : Longfellow.

neously attacked all the Austrian bailiffs, slew or drove them away, and razed their castles to the ground, after freeing their captive countrymen.

This rebellion roused the wrath of the Emperor Albert, who immediately set out from Hapsburg Castle to put it down with a heavy hand. But while crossing the Reuss, in full view of his castle and retainers, Albert was murdered by his nephew John and by four Swiss noblemen, the only persons who were with him. Then the murderers fled, leaving the emperor to breathe his last in the arms of a peasant woman who happened to be near.

It is said that, wandering among the mountains, John finally reached Tell's cottage at Bürglen, where he stopped to beg food. Here he confessed what he had done, and was sternly reproved by Tell, who proved to him that murdering a relative in revenge for personal injuries and for the sake of selfish gain, was very different from killing a tyrant in self-defence and for the good of one's country.

All but one of Albert's murderers escaped justice ; but not content with slaying that victim in the most barbarous way, his wife and daughter persecuted all the friends and relatives of those who had taken part in the crime. More than a thousand of these unfortunates are said to have perished, and it is claimed that Agnes, the emperor's daughter, personally superintended some of the executions, and rapturously exclaimed, " Now I am bathing in May dew ! " when she saw their blood flow in torrents.

On the spot where Albert died — the site of the old Roman Vindonissa — his widow and daughter erected the famous Abbey of Königsfelden, which was richly decorated with historical paintings and stained-glass windows. About two centuries later the abbey was secularised, and it is now used as an insane asylum ; but the principal objects of interest there are still shown to admiring tourists.

ALBERT was succeeded by two emperors who, not belonging to the Hapsburg race, were inclined to help the Swiss. But their brief reigns having come to an end, another Hapsburg was raised to the imperial throne, and on the 15th of November, 1315, made a determined attempt to conquer the Swiss. The latter, however, were lying in wait for his army, which they suddenly attacked while it was hemmed in between Lake Ægeri and the mountain at Morgarten. Far from expecting such an impetuous onslaught, the imperial forces, notwithstanding all their boasted panoply of war, were completely routed

by an inferior number of poorly armed patriots.
The latter, impelled by long-pent fury for all
the wrongs they had endured at the hands of
the Austrians, fairly swept them into the lake,
where many of the knights were drowned.

Ever since then, at midnight on the anniversary of the battle, it is said the lake suddenly
begins to boil, and that its seething waters as-
sume a bloody hue. Then, from the depths of
the lake, the spirits of all these drowned warriors arise, still clad in full armour and bestrid-
ing their huge battle steeds. Led by Death on
his pale horse, brandishing his scythe and hour-
glass, the dead knights march in solemn procession around the lake, plunging back into its
waters when the clocks in the neighbouring
villages strike one.

A memorial chapel, containing a painting
representing the famous encounter at Morgarten, marks the spot where the battle was fought,
and solemn anniversary services are held there
every year. This memorable victory won so
many adherents for the Swiss in their own land,
that before long the Confederation numbered
eight instead of three cantons.

Seventy years after Morgarten, the Austrians
made a second attempt to conquer the Swiss,

but they were again defeated at Sempach, on the lake of the same name, near Lucerne. At first it seemed as if this battle would prove fatal to the Swiss, for the Austrians were armed with long pikes, which enabled them to make havoc in the ranks of their opponents, whose weapons were too short to reach them.

Perceiving his companions fall around him, without being able to strike a single blow, Arnold von Winkelried suddenly determined to break the enemy's ranks. Calling loudly to his friends to look after his wife and children, this hero seized an armful of the long Austrian spears, and driving them into his own breast, fell, crying, "Make way for liberty!" His countrymen, pouring into the breach he had thus made at the expense of his life, attacked the enemy with such fury that they soon won a brilliant victory.

The battle of Sempach is commemorated by a monument, upon which stands the simple inscription: "Hier hat Winkelried den seinen eine Gasse gemacht." 1386. (Winkelried here made a way for his friends).

At Stanz, in Unterwald, the birthplace of Winkelried, a fine statue represents his heroic death. The Austrian spears clasped in a last embrace, he turns his dying glance upon his countrymen, urging them to rush over his prostrate body against their country's foe. On the anniversary of the battle a ghostly voice is heard in the castle at Richensee, dolefully calling, " Conrad ! Conrad !" In answer to this cry, a knight in black armour, with ghastly wounds in head and breast, suddenly appears on the ruined tower, and as though responding to a roll-call, gruffly answers, " Here, Austria ! "

This apparition is said to be a lord of the castle, who fell at Sempach, fighting for Austria as bravely as one of his ancestors who lost his life in that cause at Morgarten.

An outpost of the mighty Alps, Mount Pilatus, on the boundary of the cantons of Lucerne and Unterwald, is one of the most picturesque features of that region.

In the days of Roman occupation a light-house (*lucerna*) is said to have shone on the spot where the Wasserthurm now stands, and to have given its name to canton, lake, and town. At that epoch Mount Pilatus was known as Mons Fractus, Fracmont, or the Broken Mountain, owing to the jagged crag-like appearance of its summit. This descriptive name, however, was gradually supplanted by another, equally appropriate, that height — seldom free

LUCERNE, WITH MT. PILATUS.
(Old View.)

from clouds — being called Mons Pileatus, or
the Capped Mountain. Every storm coming
from the north or west gathers around this majestic peak, which serves as a natural barometer
for all the people dwelling within sight of it.
According to a very old and equally popular
rhyme, the weather probabilities are that the
day will be fair if the clouds merely rest upon
the mountain top; when they extend part way
down, it is well to be prepared for sudden
changes; but should trails of mist reach far
down Pilatus' rugged sides, it is considered an
infallible sign of a coming storm. In its oldest
form this rhyme runs : —

> " Das Wetter fein und gut
> Wann Pilatus hat 'nen Hut ;
> Trägt er einen Degen
> So gibt es Regen."

In the course of time this jingle has undergone
sundry modifications, until the English version
now reads : —

> "If Pilatus wears his cap, serene will be the day;
> If his collar he puts on, you may venture on the way;
> But if his sword he wields, at home you 'd better stay."

With the introduction of Christianity, and
the substitution of the vernacular for the Latin
language, the original meaning of *pileatus* was

entirely forgotten. The natives therefore soon began to claim that the mountain was named after Pontius Pilate, the unscrupulous governor of Judea who sentenced our Saviour to death. Little by little this belief gave rise to the picturesque legend connected with this locality, which, owing to numerous accretions, is singularly complete and interesting.

In the second century after Christ, there already existed an apocryphal Epistle of Pilate, containing his account of the trial and condemnation of Jesus Christ.[1] Warned by his wife, Procla, who had "suffered many things in a dream because of him," and by sundry miracles enumerated in his epistle, Pilate, convinced of the divine origin as well as of the innocence of the Prisoner brought before him, nevertheless weakly yielded to the threats of a few among the Jews, and condemned our Lord to an ignominious death. A moral coward, Pilate next sought to escape the natural consequences of his pusillanimous compliance by publicly washing his hands, and solemnly crying, "I am innocent of the blood of this just person ; see ye to it."

Pilate's report and various other rumours concerning the death and resurrection of Christ,

---

[1] For the Pilate legend see the author's " Legends of the Virgin and Christ."

together with frequent bitter complaints of extortion and misgovernment, finally reached the ears of Tiberius. Moved by anger and curiosity, this emperor immediately summoned the accused official to Rome to render a minute account of his stewardship. But before Pilate could reach the Eternal City, Tiberius died and was succeeded by Caligula, who, equally incensed against the faithless governor, loudly boasted that he would make very short work of his trial. The Roman courtiers were therefore seized with unbounded astonishment when they beheld their savage master treat Pontius Pilate with every mark of extreme courtesy, and heard the mild and gentle tones in which he addressed him. But no sooner had Pilate left the tribunal than all Caligula's wrath flamed up anew, and he peremptorily ordered the delinquent governor to be brought in again.

When Pilate stood before his irate judge, the latter, suddenly and mysteriously soothed, once more overwhelmed him with tokens of the highest favour instead of punishing him as he wished. The courtiers' wonder grew apace, nor did it diminish when, after Pilate's second exit, the emperor breathed forth curses and threats even more violent than before. Summoned a third time with the same baffling result, Caligula, convinced that Pilate must be protected by some amulet of great power, bade his courtiers carefully search the Judean governor ere they brought him into his presence for a fourth and last time.

In executing these orders, the courtiers discovered that Pilate wore under his usual garments the " seamless robe " of Our Lord, which he had purchased from the soldier to whom it had fallen by lot. Stripped of this talisman, Pilate stood before Caligula, who, no longer restrained from anger and vituperation by the presence of the holy relic, poured out all the vials of his wrath upon the prisoner's head, and sentenced him to an ignominious death.

To avoid the jeers of the Roman mob, and the disgrace of a public execution, Pilate is said to have committed suicide in his prison by stabbing himself with his table-knife. His corpse — as was then customary in cases of self-murder — was cast into the Tiber. But the waters, refusing to suffer such pollution, rose with unprecedented fury and overflowed their banks, while the thunder rolled, the lightning flashed, and the earth shook with such violence that all hearts were filled with awe. The terrified Romans therefore hastened to consult their oracles, and learning that the dreadful tumult was occasioned by Pilate's corpse, they quickly withdrew it from the Tiber, whose fury immediately subsided as if by magic. To dispose of the body, — which could not be buried in the usual way, — it was now cast into the Mediterranean Sea. But there, too, its presence caused such dire commotion that to ward off further misfortunes it was again removed.

Finding earth and water equally loath to harbour such an abhorred tenant, the Romans, remembering they owed a grudge to the inhabitants of Vienne, in Gaul, carefully placed Pilate's corpse upon a barge, and sent it up the Rhône. Arrived at Vienne, the Roman envoys obediently cast the body into the deepest spot in the river. But its presence there caused such damages that the frightened inhabitants hastened to forward it on to Lausanne. The same unpleasant phenomena recurring there also, Pilate's remains were finally sent out into the wilderness, far from the haunts of men. After carrying them for many days up hill and down dale, the bearers finally reached an almost inaccessible mountain. Convinced that this point was sufficiently remote from civilisation to satisfy all reasonable requirements, they cast their uncanny burden into a small lake at the foot of a barren peak, and hastened away as quickly as they could. Still, it was only with the utmost difficulty that they managed to reach

home, for no sooner had Pilate's body touched
the waters of the lonely tarn, than it stirred up
such a tempest as had never before been seen in
that region.

Night and day, year in and year out, the storm
went on raging around the lonely mountain-
top, filling with awe the hearts of the simple
peasant-folk who dwelt in the neighbouring
valleys. They too soon longed to be rid of the
unquiet spirit, but could find no people willing
to harbour a ghost which raged round the mountain, waded about the lake until it overflowed,
stormed up and down the jagged rocks howling
with fear and remorse, and which occasionally
indulged in fearful wrestling-bouts with the spirit
of King Herod, or those of other famous male-
factors. Even in his comparatively quiet moments, Pilate was dreaded, for then he sat aloft
on the Güppe, — one of the peaks of the mountain, — grimly conjuring new storms, washing
his hands in the dripping clouds, and shaking
huge rain-drops from his trembling fingers down
upon the fertile pastures below him. None of the
shepherds dared venture near him, because he
stampeded their flocks by his violent gestures,
and often hurled cows and goats over the precipices and down on the sharp rocks, where they
were dashed to pieces

Years, therefore, passed by without Pilate's being molested in any way; but at last there came a travelling scholar, who, having mastered the Black Art at Salamanca, was fully competent to deal with spirits of all kinds. The people no sooner heard of his unusual accomplishments than they crowded around him, eagerly imploring him to cast a quieting spell upon Pilate's restless ghost, and proffering rich rewards if he would only put an end to their woes.

Thus urged, the magician consented to try his skill. Journeying up the mountain, he came, after several hours of hard climbing, to the foot of the peak upon which Pontius Pilate sat watching his approach with lowering brows. Placing himself upon a large stone, the conjurer drew a magic circle around him, and then began his incantations. But even his most powerful formulas left Pilate unmoved, although they made the rocks around him quiver and shake as if about to fall. When the magician perceived this, he changed his position to a peak directly opposite the one Pilate had chosen for his favourite seat, and undismayed by his first failure, again began reciting all the most potent exorcisms he knew. This time they were not without effect, for Pilate suddenly rose in anger

from his rocky throne and rushed toward the intruder as if to sweep him off the face of the
earth.   But balked of this amiable intention
by the magic circle, instead of whisking the magician off into space, Pilate could only rage
around and around him, trampling the ground
with such fury that no grass can even now grow
on that spot.   Indeed, his mere footprints laid
such a curse upon the soil that no dew has
fallen upon it, nor any animal ventured to cross
it since that day !

After careering thus wildly around the scholar
for some time, Pilate's ghost, weakening per-
ceptibly, finally agreed to retire to the tarn high
up the mountain side.   There he promised to
remain in peace, provided no one wantonly disturbed his rest, and he was allowed to range the
mountain at will one day in the year.

The exorcist having consented to this stipula-
tion, Pilate further proved he had not sojourned
among the Jews in vain, by carefully bargaining
that a steed should be provided to bear him off
in state to his last resting-place.   The Salamancan scholar therefore called up from the depths
a flame-breathing steed of the blackest hue,
which bore Pontius Pilate off at a truly infernal
pace.   As they dashed over the rocks, the
steed's clattering hoofs struck out so many

sparks that the mountain was illumined from base to summit, and it stamped so hard that the marks of its flying feet can still be seen in the rocks near the tarn.

Arriving there, Pontius Pilate vanished in the depths of the lake, or morass, where he quietly stayed, thus honestly keeping his part of the agreement. Since then, unless disturbed by sceptics coming to mock at him, or cast sticks and stones into his retreat, Pilate has quietly reposed in the depths of his lake. But although sure to resent any mark of disrespect, by rising to stir up a fearful storm, his spirit has always been sufficiently discriminating to make no demonstration when his rest is broken by accident or through ignorance.

Such was the dread of rousing Pilate's wrath, that the magistrates of Lucerne solemnly issued a decree forbidding all strangers to visit the tarn. They also made all the herdsmen take a yearly oath not to guide any foreigner thither, or to point out the road which led there. Any infringement of this edict was punished with the utmost severity, as can still be seen in the annals of Lucerne ; and the law remained in force until 1585, the time of the Reformation.

Then a doughty pastor prevailed upon the magistrates to repeal their edict, and climbed up to the tarn.   There he convinced all the people that there was no further cause for their super- stitious fears, by flinging stones into the water, calling out every imaginable insult, and boldly challenging Pilate's ghost to rise and do its worst.

Pilate's spirit, banned by the Salamancan student, has ever since been said to rise only on Good Friday.   Clad in purple, he then sits upon a judgment seat, which comes up out of the lake, and repeats in pantomime the actions he performed on the fatal and memorable day when he sentenced Christ to the cross.   Then, too, Pilate always washes his shaking hands, in the futile effort to cleanse himself from all share in that deadly sin ; and any wanderer who, by choice or accident, gazes at his distorted features at that time is sure to die within the year.   On Good Friday, too, Pilate often rages around the mountain in despairing remorse, but at mid- night he invariably sinks down again into his morass.

There are numerous variations of this legend, one of which claims that Pilate ruled in Vienne, where he committed suicide by casting himself into the Rhône.   Another version says that, full of remorse for his crime, he wandered from place to place, until in despair he finally drowned himself in the lake on the mountain bearing his name.

Such was the terror inspired by this mountain, and the difficulty of reaching its summit, that the first ascension is said to have taken place only in 1518. As one can seldom obtain a clear view even after bearing the fatigue of such an arduous climb, it was rarely visited by strangers until the wonderful railway was built which now enables travellers to reach its top with the utmost ease. Since then Mount Pilatus has become a favourite goal for excursions, and those who have once beheld the extensive panorama visible from its crest can never forget the marvellous view, which, extending as far as the eye can reach, includes glaciers, mountains, valleys, streams, and lakes, not to mention picturesque towns, villages, churches, and castles, which abound in that section of the country.

BESIDES the legend from which Mount Pilatus is popularly supposed to have derived its name, many others are told relating to various points on the mountain. For instance, it is said that a cooper from Lucerne once climbed up its rocky sides in quest of wood for barrel hoops and staves, and fell into a deep gully whose sides were so high and steep that he could not

get out of it again.   The soil at the bottom was
so soft and slimy that the cooper, uninjured by
his fall, next tried to make his way out by
following the bottom of this cleft.   He could
find no issue, however, but finally came to a
sort of tunnel in the rocks.   Entering boldly,
he suddenly found himself face to face with a
couple of huge, fire-breathing dragons.   A hasty
sign of the cross, and a fervent, if trembling
prayer for the Virgin's protection, effectively
closed the mouths of the dragons already gaping
wide to devour him, and transformed them into
gentle creatures which fawned upon him, humbly licking his hands and feet.   Their manners
were so ingratiating that the cooper soon
ceased to fear them, and sitting down beside
them, spent six months in their company, feed-
ing as they did upon a salty substance which
exuded from a crack in the rocks.

Winter over, the dragons, who had lain supine
in the cave all that time, wriggled slowly out
into the gorge, where they began stretching
and shaking themselves, spreading and furling
their wings, as if to make sure their pliancy had
not suffered from a long period of inaction.
Then the amazed cooper suddenly beheld one of
the monsters rise straight up into the air, and
once out of the deep cleft, fly in wide circles

far above his head and finally pass out of sight.

The second dragon soon after showing signs of a desire to follow its mate, the cooper promptly grasped it by the tail, and was whisked up out of the abyss, but gently set down again on a soft grass plot near the city of Lucerne. On entering that town, he was rapturously welcomed by his friends, who, after vainly seeking him on the mountain, had given him up as dead.

In token of gratitude for his marvellous preservation, and safe return to his native city, the cooper gave a communion service to the church of St. Leodegarius in 1420. On this service is a quaint representation of his adventure with the dragons on Mount Pilatus. The legend declares, however, that, unable to digest common viands after living so long upon the dragons' mysterious food, the cooper died of starvation two months after his return to Lucerne.

ANOTHER legend claims that a peasant from Lucerne once beheld a dragon rise slowly from the Rigi and fly heavily towards Mount Pilatus. Gazing in open-mouthed astonishment at this wonderful sight, the peasant next saw the monster drop something, and when sufficiently recovered from his terror to investigate what it might be, he discovered it was a huge clot of blood in which lay imbedded a precious stone.

This jewel was found in time to possess wonderful curative powers, for a mere touch of it healed victims of the pest and of other equally fatal diseases. The Dragonstone was, therefore, carefully preserved in the city, where it can still be seen, although for some time past its medicinal powers are said to have deserted it.

WHILE the summit of Mount Pilatus is quite barren, the lower slopes provide pasture for large herds of cows and goats which graze there under the care of their herdsmen. One of the highest and finest pastures is the Bründlisalp, near which is a cave known as the Dominik-höhle or Dominican's Grotto. A huge rock bearing the rough semblance of a human form stands at the entrance to this cave.

According to tradition, a mountain giant was once posted in this grotto to keep watch over the region round about, and give the people due notice of the approach of any foe. When an enemy drew near, he gave the alarm; then, placing himself at the head of the natives, attacked the foe with such strength and fury that he always secured the victory for his country.

But a day finally came when the *Swiss*, who had never borne arms except to defend themselves against the incursions of strangers, suddenly found themselves unable to agree, and resorting to force, began a civil war. Feeling strife in the air, the giant rushed out of his cave to ascertain what was the matter. But when he beheld brother armed against brother, saw the Swiss attack each other with rage, and viewed their blood flow in torrents, he was so horror-struck that his cry died on his lips, his blood froze in his veins, and he stood there immovable, turned into stone! Ever since then, the petrified giant at the entrance of the Dominican Cave is pointed out as an emblem of patriotism and as a solemn warning against civil strife.

MOUNT PILATUS is said to have long been the home of countless little gnomes who hid in every nook and crevice and under every stone. These dwarfs were about eighteen inches high, and wore long green mantles to conceal the fact that they had goose-shaped feet. Bright red caps were jauntily perched on top of their snow-white hair, while long beards of the same colour flowed down over their breasts. The gnomes not only watched over the chamois, bounding from rock to rock, but tended the fish sporting in the depths of the mountain streams, and protected all game from the greed of wanton sportsmen.

These gnomes were so obliging that they cheerfully helped the herdsmen watch and tend their cattle, milk the cows, make butter or cheese, and in exchange for their manifold services merely required a small bowlful of milk or cream. Gentle and helpful as long as they were treated kindly, the gnomes were sure to revenge themselves upon any mortals who ill-treated them or their protégés, or hurt their feelings by trying to get a sight of their misshapen feet.

A rich peasant once pastured his cattle high up on the beautiful Kastelnalp, on Mount Pilatus, where the grass was so rich that the cows had to be milked three times a day. Magdalen, the only daughter of a widowed cousin, once painfully made her way up to this alp to beg for a little help for her sick mother, who had neither food nor medicine in the house. The rich man, who had provisions in plenty, and who stored away cheese after cheese in his cellars, nevertheless refused to help his poor relatives, and sent Magdalen home empty-handed and in tears.

Overtaken on her way down the mountain by a sudden thunder-storm, the girl sought shelter in the hut of her lover, a herdsman to whom she confided all her sorrows. A generous, noble-hearted fellow, Alois no sooner heard of his sweetheart's destitution and disappointment than he ran to get a small cheese, the only food he had in the house, and forced her to accept it for her starving mother. The storm over, Magdalen set out again with lightened heart, but her foot suddenly slipping on the wet grass, she let go the precious cheese, which, bounding from rock to rock, rolled over the edge of a precipice, into whose depths it disappeared.

Magdalen's tears now flowed afresh ; but while she sat there wringing her hands in despair, she suddenly felt a twitch at her dress. Looking down, she there beheld one of the tiny mountain spirits, carrying a small cheese upon his shoulder, and holding a bundle of medicinal herbs in his hand.

" Weep no longer," the little man gently said. " The hard-hearted owner of the Kastelnalp shall be duly punished for his refusal to help you. In the meantime take these herbs, which will restore your mother's health, and I am sure both you and she will enjoy this cheese."

The little man then vanished, leaving his gifts behind him, and Magdalen hastened joyfully home. Her first care was to prepare herb tea for the patient, whose health was miraculously restored as soon as she had tasted it. But when Magdalen tried to cut the cheese the kind-hearted gnome had given her, she was amazed to find it was a solid lump of pure gold! She and her mother were so rich with this treasure that they soon purchased the Bründlisalp, where Magdalen and Alois, a happy husband and wife, tended their flocks together.

As for the hard-hearted owner of the Kasteln-alp, he was justly punished for his lack of charity. The sudden rain-storm, loosening the rocks above his pasture, started a landslide which covered his alp with such a mass of loose stones that not a blade of grass has ever been seen on it since. Besides this, a fragment of rock struck the owner as he fled, and breaking both his legs, left him so badly crippled that he never walked without crutches again.

As picturesque as Mount Pilatus, although in a different way, and far more accessible for pedestrians, the Rigi has long been a centre of

THE RIGI.

attraction for travellers from all parts of the
world. Before the two railways were built,
which now carry passengers up to the mountain-
top in less than an hour and a half, ascensions
were frequently made on foot or on horseback.
This climb was cheerfully undertaken in hopes
of enjoying the marvellous views obtainable from
many points on the mountain, and the vast panorama, with changing hues at sunset and sunrise,
which can best be seen from the mountain's crest.

The slopes of the Rigi are now all covered
with orchards and rich pastures, for although
snow frequently falls on its summit even in mid-
summer, it never lingers there long, owing to the
warm rays of the sun striking directly upon it.
There are countless points of interest to be seen
on this mountain, but the most characteristic of
all its legends is connected with the gushing
spring of ice-cold water at Rigi-Kaltbad.

We are told that in the days when Austrian
bailiffs still exercised their tyranny over the land,
three lovely sisters dwelt in the Arth valley at
the foot of the Rigi. Not content with despoil-
ing these defenceless maidens of all their worldly
goods, the bailiff of Schwanau, although aware
that they loathed him, persecuted them with his
unwelcome attentions, and even attempted to
rob them of their honour.

In their terror lest they should become victims
of this evil man's lust, the sisters fled from Arth
one night, and boldly rushed into the dense forest which then covered all the slopes of the mountain.   The wild beasts abounding in that region
seemed to these helpless maidens far less to be
dreaded than the human beast whose pursuit they
were trying to escape.   They therefore bravely
threaded their way up the Rigi by the dim light
of the stars, nor paused in their flight until they
reached a sheltered plateau high up on the
mountain.

Exposed to the southern sun, and provided
with a spring of crystalline water flowing plenti-
fully from the rocks near by, this place seemed so
remote from mankind, and so fitted by nature to
serve as a safe retreat, that the three sisters determined to spend the rest of their lives there.   They
therefore built a little hut of bark stripped from
the trunks of fallen trees and of wattled branches,
and gathering moss for their beds, spent summer
and winter there in utter seclusion.   The ber-
ries and edible roots collected on the mountain
side were their only food, while the sparkling
water from the fountain served as their sole bev-
erage.   In their gratitude for escaping from their
cruel persecutor, the sisters, who had always
been remarkable for their piety, spent most of

their days and part of their nights in praising God for their deliverance, fervently praying that they might live and die in the service of their Maker.

Although entirely cut off from mankind, — for no one ever ventured so far up the mountain then, — and notwithstanding the cold and the other privations they had to endure, the sisters dwelt here year after year, without a murmur over their hard fate. Such was their piety, that the angels kept constant watch over them, and finally bore their sinless souls to heaven, leaving three lambent flames to hover over their tenantless bodies.

In the meantime no one knew what had become of the three girls who had vanished so mysteriously from the Arth valley, and their former friends, gazing up at Mount Rigi, little suspected that those tender maidens were even then living like hermits far above their heads. When the sisters died, however, the miraculous lights hovering over their bodies were distinctly perceived from various parts of the lake and valley, greatly rousing the curiosity of all who saw them. Night after night the lights twinkled up there in undiminished brightness, until the stars paled and the sun rose, flooding mountain, lake, and valley with its golden beams.

Thinking some holy hermit must have built

his cell up there, and wishing to satisfy their
curiosity as well as secure his blessing, some
herdsmen determined to make their way up the
mountain in spite of pathless forests and dense
undergrowth.   After a long and arduous climb,
they finally reached the plateau, where they
were amazed to find a hut showing signs of prolonged occupation, but now fast falling into
ruins.   In searching for further traces of the
supposed hermit, they suddenly discovered the
bodies lying side by side near the ever-flowing
spring, and beheld the three flames float slowly
upward and vanish into the blue sky.

Awed by this miracle, the herdsmen reverently buried the three corpses, and over the spot
where they rested, built a rustic chapel which
was first dedicated to the Virgin Mary and then
to the archangel St. Michael.   A church now
stands on this hallowed spot, which is frequently
visited by pilgrims, as well as by those who
come to Rigi-Kaltbad for health or for pleasure.
The spring, which still gushes from the rock, was
long known as the Schwesternborn, in memory
of the pious sisters, whose sinless lives and death
cast a glamour of romance over that spot.

THE ruins of the Castle of Schwanau, on the
island of the same name, in the Lake of Lowertz,

at the foot of the Rigi, are connected with the above legend, because here lived the cruel persecutor from whom the pious sisters fled. Not content with driving these girls away from home, the Lord of Schwanau once kidnapped a maiden from Arth, whom he carried by force into this castle, where she vainly tried to escape from his clutches. This lady, however, was not entirely destitute of male protectors, and when her brothers heard how she had been treated, they sallied forth in anger and slew her ravisher. Then calling the freemen of Schwyz to their aid, they captured and destroyed the castle, leaving it a mass of smoking ruins, with only one tower standing to serve as a monument of the Lord of Schwanau's crimes and of their revenge.

It is said that although the cruel kidnapper was slain nearly six hundred years ago, his spirit can still find no rest. Every year, at midnight, on the anniversary of the day when the frantic girl rushed wildly through the castle to escape his pursuit, a flash of lightning and a deep roll of thunder herald his return to the scene of his crime. Suddenly he appears in the midst of the ruins, where he stands, quaking with fear, until a maiden, clad in white and bearing a flaming torch, rushes out of the tower. Then the bailiff utters a blood-curdling cry of terror, and turning. races madly from one part of the castle to the other. closely pursued by his innocent victim. Over crumbling stones, up and down the ruined tower, through former passages and along ruined battlements, pursuer and pursued hasten with flying steps, until, seeing no other hope of escape, the Lord of Schwanau, with a last mad shriek, plunges from the parapet into the lake, whose dark waters close with a dull splash over his head. Then the avenging maiden vanishes, not to be seen again until the hour strikes when she must once more sally forth to torture the bailiff for his heinous crime.

ANOTHER legend, also connected with the Lake of Lowertz, claims that a church once stood very near the edge of the water. There, while the women and children of the neighbourhood knelt within its holy precincts, Sunday after Sunday, dutifully reciting their prayers, the men sat on the church steps, smoking, drinking, and gambling. Such was their lack of respect for religion and the divine service, that they even swore out loud, and flung their dice down upon the stones with such violence that the noise often drowned all sounds of prayer and praise.

These wicked men, who mocked at the priest whenever he tried to make them change their evil ways, were, however, to be sorely punished for their sacrilegious behaviour. One Sunday, while gambling on the church steps as usual, a sudden storm swept over the little lake, and before they could gather up their dice or scramble to their feet, a huge wave swept right over their heads. At the same moment the church sank down into the depths of the lake, where it still lies many fathoms under water. Some of the local boatmen claim that the top of the church spire can still be seen when the water is clear, and that at the wonted hour for worship the bells can always be heard ringing a soft and musical peal. Then the sound of prayer and praise becomes faintly audible, and very keen ears can distinguish a rattle of dice and muttered oaths. The women and children are said to be perfectly happy in their endless adoration, but the men are compelled to continue for ever the sacrilegious game which has become prolonged and unbearable torture.

LEAVING the city of Stanz and going up the Aa valley, toward the Titlis, which forms the boundary between the cantons of Uri and Bern, you pass Engelberg, and the Sürenen-alp, of which the following characteristic legends are told.

Count Conrad von Seldenbüren, in a moment of great danger, made a solemn vow that he would build a monastery should he escape unharmed. Saved from his imminent peril, he immediately prepared to keep his promise, and with that purpose in view, set out with a number of his friends and retainers to select a site for the projected building.

Riding along the valley, he drew rein from time to time to admire the lovely landscape, and to inhale the perfumed breezes wafted down from the surrounding mountains. There were so many charming spots that Conrad, quite bewildered by the choice, finally breathed a fervent inward prayer for divine guidance. Looking up a moment later, he suddenly beheld an angel host sweep down through the blue sky. They alighted on a neighbouring eminence, where the celestial choir intoned a hymn of praise, their voices faintly reaching Conrad's ear and filling his heart with ineffable bliss.

The hymn ended, the angels again rose up into heaven; but Conrad, overjoyed by the miracle vouchsafed him, loudly declared that not only should the monastery be built on the hill upon which the angels had rested, but that it should ever after be known as the Engelberg, or Angels' Mountain.

Founded in 1119, the Engelberg Abbey soon became rich and prosperous, for the monks owned all the pastures around there, and had so many head of cattle that they stored away countless cheeses in their great cellars. The choicest of all their grazing grounds were, however, on the Sürenenalp, where they sent their herdsmen with their finest cattle.

One of these men is said to have developed a special affection for a silvery-white sheep entrusted to his care, which followed him wherever he went, and so became a great pet. His fondness for the creature became such that he finally baptized it with holy water stolen from the monastery chapel. He did this, hoping to preserve it from all harm ; but no sooner was the sacrilegious ceremony accomplished than the silvery-fleeced sheep, transformed into a raging monster, fiercely attacked shepherds and flocks, and drove them away from the rich pastures. Such was the fear inspired by this creature — which no weapon could wound — that the peasants, one and all, refused to venture up the mountain, and even the much frequented Sürenen Pass was entirely deserted.

The monks of Engelberg, unable to use their pastures themselves, or to derive any income by renting them out to others, finally sold them

for a mere song to the people of Uri. The
latter, thrifty in the extreme, could not bear the
thought that the fine grass on the Sürenenalp
was going to waste, so they tried various devices
to kill or capture the demoniacal sheep. Weapons, prayers, and exorcisms proving equally unavailing, they finally bespoke the good offices
of a travelling scholar, who had studied the
Black Art under no less capable an instructor
than Satan himself.

After sundry liberal potations of the warm
southern wine brought by the Urners from Italy
over the famous St. Gothard and Furka passes,
and after duly securing a pocketful of gold, the
magician gave the people minute directions,
assuring them that if carefully carried out they
would settle the obnoxious sheep for ever.

By his directions, the Urners selected a snow-
white bull, which was fed with the milk of one
cow during the first year, and with that of two
during the second. Increasing the rations of
this animal at the rate of a cow per year, the
bull in the ninth year was consuming the entire
produce of nine cows, and had grown to a
prodigious size.

The ninth year ended, a virgin from Atting-
hausen, carefully arrayed in bridal white, was
told to lead the chosen bull to the Sürenenalp.

Her little hand passed through the ring set in the bull's nose, this maiden slowly wended her way up the mountain, followed by the bull, which obeyed her slightest touch. When they reached the choicest pasture, the maiden suddenly let go her charge, for the monster sheep stood very near and about to attack her. At the same moment the bull thundered past her with lowered horns, and rushing toward the christened sheep began a terrible fight. The mountain shook and groaned beneath the trampling feet of the animals, which wrestled together with locked horns, while black clouds loomed up over the pasture, blotting out the bright sunshine, and making the air oppressively hot and close.

The darkness soon grew so intense that the people in the valley could no longer distinguish either trembling maiden or struggling monsters. All at once a dazzling flash of lightning rent the black clouds asunder, and it was instantly followed by a peal of thunder so loud and prolonged that the peasants, ducking their heads between their knees in terror, tightly closed their eyes.

When they again ventured to look up, they fairly gasped with amazement, for the blue sky again arched above the alp, the storm clouds

were rapidly drifting away, and golden sunbeams
flooded the spot where bull and sheep had met.

No trace of cattle or maiden being visible,
the peasants, after some hesitation, timidly ventured up the mountain to see what had become
of both. On the grass they found a bloody
and trampled mound of flesh, which upon investigation proved to be the remains of the
accursed sheep, but the maiden had vanished
for ever, leaving no trace. On the banks of
the Aawasser, quite near its source, they further
discovered the body of the snow-white bull,
which, having drank too greedily of the ice-cold
waters while overheated from his exertions, had
met with a sudden but natural death.

Since then, the place where the bull expired
has been known as the Bull's Stream, or the
Steersbrook, and cows, sheep, and goats have
feasted unmolested upon the luscious pastures
on the Sürenenalp. Besides, in grateful recognition for the white bull's services, the people
of Uri placed his head upon a shield, decreeing
that ever after the head of a bull should grace
the official seal of the canton of Uri and form
its sole coat of arms.

At the northern extremity of the canton of
Uri, and at the point where the Lake of Lucerne

makes a sudden southward bend, rises the Seelisberg, renowned alike for its beautiful scenery and rich pastures. Here once dwelt a peasant who, having won the good-will of the mountain dwarfs, often received their help. The herdsman, in return for their favours, lavished upon them the best of all he had, and when called away by urgent business, often left them in charge of chalet and herd.

The mountain dwarfs could always be trusted to see to everything, provided the Föhn, or south wind, did not blow. But whenever the breath of that strong wind swept over the glaciers, they one and all crept far down into the bowels of the earth; whence they did not emerge until it ceased to rage.

Once, while the herdsman was on the opposite side of the lake, the Föhn suddenly broke loose with such fury that although he made frantic efforts to cross the water, it was four whole days before the waves subsided enough to enable him to return home. During all that time the dwarfs had cowered down in the depths of the earth; so nearly all the cattle had perished from hunger and thirst. When the peasant entered his stables and saw this sad state of affairs, he tore his hair, and in his despair even cursed his little friends. The latter, who in ordinary times would have resented the slightest approach to bad language, patiently bore all his reviling, and when he was somewhat cooler, offered to teach him the art of making cheese from sweet milk. This would enable him to use much produce generally lost because it did not thicken in time for use.

The herdsmen, on hearing this offer, reluctantly admitted that if it were possible to make cheese from sweet milk, he might yet retrieve his fortunes. So the dwarfs bade him kill his old goat, showed him how to curdle milk by using its stomach, as rennet, and taught him to make the excellent cheese for which the Seelisberg is still noted. Thanks to the secret revealed by the repentant dwarfs, the peasant soon became rich again, and when he died at a good old age, he left behind him fine pastures, countless heads of cattle, and the invaluable receipt which he had learned from his little friends, and which his descendants still use.

In going over the Klausen Pass, and in crossing the boundary of the cantons of Glarus and Uri, one is reminded of the famous old quarrel concerning this frontier. Both cantons once claimed the best pastures along it, and as the herdsmen often came to blows over this matter, it was finally arranged to settle the dispute once for all.

The jury before whom the matter was laid, composed of the most honest and influential citizens in both cantons, decreed that as the matter could not be settled satisfactorily otherwise, it should be decided by a race. According to their minute directions, each canton was to select a cock and a champion. On an appointed day, at their respective cocks' first crow, these champions were to start from Altorf and the Linth valley, and running with all their might, fix the boundary line for ever on the spot where they finally met. This wise decree pleased both cantons ; cocks and champions were duly chosen, and the day for the race was eagerly expected.

The people of Glarus, thinking their rooster would be most likely to wake early if well fed and tended, lavished every care upon him, while those of Uri kept theirs half starved, declaring he would sleep little if hungry and thirsty.

When fall came and the time appointed for the race, the Urner's conjectures proved correct, for their skinny rooster awoke at the very first gleam of dawn. His hoarse crow had scarcely been uttered, when their champion set out from Altorf for his race to the frontier.

Over in Glarus, however, matters were less promising, for while all the people of the Linth valley stood in expectant silence around their cock, he slept on and on, until all the changing tints of dawn had coloured the sky in turn, and the sun rose triumphant above the horizon. Then he gave a lusty crow ; but although the Glarus champion ran his best, he had set out so long after his rival that he soon saw him coming rapidly down the Grat.

When they met, the Urner triumphantly cried : " Here is the boundary ! "

But the Glarner, pleading for his community, said : " Neighbour, I pray thee, be so just as to grant me a bit of the fine pasture land thou hast acquired by good luck."

At first the Urner would not consent, but as his antagonist continued to plead with gentle importunity, he finally exclaimed : " Well, friend, thou shalt have as much ground as thou canst carry me over ! "

The overjoyed man from Glarus now picked up his opponent, and although the latter was heavy, and the road led up a steep hill, toiled valiantly onward until he sank down lifeless far up the slope. By his heroic efforts this man thus won a considerable piece of pasture land for his fellow-citizens, who, in grateful memory of his efforts in their behalf, buried him on the spot where he fell, and still speak of his feat of strength with wonder and admiration.

THE marvellous St. Gothard Railway, which cost ten years of persistent labour, crosses almost countless tunnels and bridges, and gives the traveller an opportunity to see some of the finest and wildest scenery in the world. At Altorf it passes the Capuchin Monastery, in connection with which the following story is told.

The monks, in olden times, lived on a very friendly footing with the people all around there, until one of them, meeting a pretty girl on a lonely path, declared he must have the bunch of Alpine flowers she wore on her breast, and a kiss besides. The peasant maiden, who had picked the flowers for her lover, and who was far from expecting such behaviour on the part of one of the monks, gave a loud shriek when he attempted to secure the bouquet and salute her by force.

At the same instant the ground shook, a wide crevice appeared, whence rose a cloud of smoke. Then a slip knot suddenly closed around the neck of the monk, who was dragged down into the abyss, which closed over him with an ominous crash! Since then, if we are to believe the chronicles, no monk from the Capuchin convent has ever dared raise his eyes to any of the girls of the town, or to exchange even a conventional greeting with them.

One of the tunnels crossed by the railroad, is near a ravine which is known as the Pfaffensprung or the Monk's Leap, and owes its name to the following legend. A wicked monk once kidnapped a young girl, and was fleeing with her through the mountains, when he suddenly discovered that he was pursued. To escape from his would-be captors, and retain possession of the girl he had carried off, this monk ran to the edge of the Reuss. There, seizing her in his arms, he took a desperate leap, and — helped by the Devil — landed safely on the other side! According to some versions of the story, the monk was none other than the Evil One himself, for it is claimed no one else could have leaped across a chasm which measures no less than twenty-two feet at this place.

The old-fashioned stage road which winds its way over the St. Gothard, passes through Schoellenen, Goeschenen (the entrance to the St. Gothard tunnel), and over the new Devil's

Bridge. This is built across the Reuss at a point where steep rocks tower above and below it on all sides, and where the scenery is extremely wild and impressive.

From the new bridge one can see the remains of a more ancient structure, of which the following legend is told, as well as of all old bridges built in dangerous or difficult places, such as that of Pont-la-Ville over the Sarine in Fribourg, and the one in the ravine of the Morge in the Valais.

Already in very olden times the people of Uri had discovered that if they could only establish a safe road over the St. Gothard mountain they would be able to earn many a penny by trading with Italy. They therefore spared neither pains nor expense, and built one foot after another of the road, even piercing the hard rock in one spot to make what is still known as the Urner Loch, or Hole of Uri. Countless apparently insurmountable obstacles were gradually overcome, and the road, which had been begun on both sides of the mountain, was rapidly drawing close together near the banks of Reuss. There, however, the builders paused appalled on either bank, for it seemed quite impossible to bridge the awful chasm near the falls.

A meeting was therefore called at Goeschenen,

where, although there was no lack of talking,
smoking, and drinking, no satisfactory decision
could be reached. A stranger, clad in black,
with broad-brimmed hat and bold heron feather,
sat at a neighbouring table and listened attentively to this discussion. Finally, seeing the
meeting about to break up, he drew near the
talkers, and taking a seat beside the principal
magistrate in front of the fire, announced that
he was a famous builder, and could span the
stream before morning. He even offered to
show them a fine bridge there at dawn, on the
next day, provided they were willing to pay his
price.

One and all now exclaimed that nothing he
could ask would seem too much, so the stranger
in black quickly responded, —

" Very well, then, it is a bargain ! To-mor-
row you shall have your bridge, but in payment
I shall claim the first living creature which passes
over it. Here is my hand upon it ! "

Saying these words, he seized the hand of the
astonished magistrate beside him, and before any
one could add another word, disappeared. The
people gazed at one another in silence for a
moment, then made furtive signs of the cross.
As soon as the chief magistrate could speak,
he loudly declared the stranger must be his

Satanic Majesty in person! In support of this assertion, he declared that the stranger, while sitting in front of the fire, had boldly thrust his feet right into the red-hot coals, where he kept them while talking, as if the heat were agreeable to him; and added that he had distinctly felt sharp claws when the man in black shook hands with him to close the bargain.

All now shuddered with fear, and a general wail of terror arose. But a tailor who was present at the meeting, promptly bade his fellow-citizens fear naught, for he would settle the bill with their architect on the morrow. This offer was gladly accepted, the meeting was speedily dissolved, and all hastened home, because none of them cared to be out after dark while still under the spell of their recent encounter with the Spirit of Evil. That night no one slept in the neighbourhood, for although the sky had been clear when they went to bed, a sudden storm arose and raged with fury until morning.

Amid the roll of thunder, incessant flashes of vivid lightning, and violent gusts of wind, they heard the splitting and falling of rocks, which seemed to roll all the way down the steep mountain side and crash into the valley. But when morning came, no signs of storm were left, and as soon as the sun had risen and they again dared venture out, all rushed forth in a body to see what had happened. When they drew near the Reuss, they could not sufficiently express their wonder and admiration, for a fine stone bridge arched boldly over the swift stream.

On the opposite side stood the black-garbed stranger, grinning fiendishly and encouraging the people by word and gesture to test his bridge by walking across it. Just then the tailor appeared, carrying a large bag. He advanced as if to cross first, but instead of setting foot upon the structure, deftly opened his bag, from which escaped rats and mice, closely followed by a few cats.

The Devil, for it was he, gave a yell of rage when he saw himself thus outwitted, and, forgetting the part he had played until then, cast off his disguise and ran down Goeschenen for a huge rock, which he intended to hurl at the bridge so as to wreck it entirely before any other living creature could cross.

On his way back, however, Satan met a little old woman, who, frightened by his black looks, made a sign of the cross which caused him to drop his burden and beat a hasty retreat into his own realm. To this day, however, the people still point out the huge boulder in which

THE DEVIL'S BRIDGE.

the marks of Satan's claws are still visible, and which is known as the Devil's Stone.

According to another version, the Devil no sooner saw himself outwitted than he seized handfuls of rock which he hurled at the bridge. But these missiles were all deflected by a cross which the tailor planted in the middle of the structure as soon as the animals reached the other side. These big stones now lie scattered in the bed of the Reuss, and around the pillars of the bridge, where, to the Devil's constant chagrin, they only serve to strengthen his construction.

To avenge himself in a slight measure, however, the Evil One posted one of his own imps in this valley. When travellers pass, this demon pounces down upon them unseen, snatches their hats off their heads, and with a slight mocking whistle tosses them into the middle of the stream. This imp, known as the Hat Fiend, or Hut Schelm, still haunts the valley, although centuries have passed since the Devil played the part of engineer for the people of Uri.

A JUDGE of Bellinzona, known far and wide for his unswerving honesty, was wont to ride daily to Magadino to attend court there and mete out strict justice to all who appeared before him.

Although this was long years ago, when most judges openly accepted bribes, this particular magistrate could never be bought, and while the innocent loudly praised him, all wrong-doers hated him cordially.

Confirmed thieves and habitual criminals were particularly angry at his mode of procedure ; so they finally decided it would be well to waylay the upright judge one dark night on his homeward journey, and end his blameless career by a foul murder.

Three young men therefore registered a solemn oath to kill the magistrate, and posting themselves in ambush behind the rocks by the roadside, they impatiently awaited the appearance of their victim. Toward midnight a clatter of hoofs was heard on the stony pathway, and the lurking assassins, peering cautiously forth, beheld the judge galloping toward them, preceded and followed by three armed horsemen. The three highwaymen, who had expected to see the judge alone or in company of one servant only, feeling loath to attack a force so superior to their own, allowed the judge to pass by unmolested, and postponed their attempt until the morrow. Then, reinforced by six of their evil companions, they again lay in wait for the incorruptible magistrate.

But instead of rushing out to attack him as soon as he drew near, they cowered low in fear, for their expected victim was escorted by a troop of twelve armed men, riding six before and six behind him. The crime was deferred by unanimous if tacit consent until the next day, when six more ruffians joined the murderers, to accomplish their wicked purpose without further delay.

Again they waited and listened, and again their hearts beat fast at the sound of approaching horsemen ; but their hands dropped powerless to their sides on perceiving the judge ride rapidly past them with an escort of twenty-four men !

Convinced that their plans had been revealed to the man they hated, the murderers now resolved to follow him home, to discover which men formed his body-guard, and if possible to find the informer or at least secure the connivance of the horsemen by means of large bribes. They therefore noiselessly pursued the little cavalcade, and saw it come to a sudden halt in front of the judge's house. There the magistrate slowly dismounted, gave the bridle of his weary steed to a waiting servant, and entered his house without saying a word or making a sign to the horsemen standing all around him.

As the door slammed shut, the servant led the horse away to the stable, and the mounted escort suddenly vanished into thin air. Then only, the amazed highwaymen became aware that the judge had been guarded by angelic spirits, detailed to watch over his safety, but of whose presence he was evidently not aware. This discovery filled their hearts with such awe that they never again attempted to lay violent hands upon him ; but one of their number, overcome by remorse, finally went to seek him, and confessing their evil intentions, humbly begged his pardon for the projected crime.

The judge, who was as merciful as he was just, freely forgave this man ; but, relying upon divine protection in case of need, he continued to mete out justice as before, and rode home alone when his day's work was over.   No harm ever befell him, and it is said that when his upright career on earth was ended, the invisible body-guard escorted him to the great tribunal, where the verdict awarded to him was: " Well done, thou good and faithful servant, enter thou into the joy of thy Lord."

16

SCHAFFHAUSEN

IN olden times, when the Alemans first invaded Switzerland, they practised the bloody rites of their religion at the Falls of the Rhine, near Schaffhausen, and sacrificed many white horses to the god of the Rhine. These steeds were driven into the water some distance above the cataract, and in spite of their frantic efforts were swept over the brink by the rapid current.

Not long ago, horse-shoes could still be seen in the cracks of the rocks near the waterfall, and even now, on moonlight nights or on misty days, the ghosts of these sacrificed steeds can still be seen, rearing and plunging in the waters, and wildly tossing their snow-white manes. These wraiths are most clearly discerned during the night from Friday to Saturday, because it was then that they were offered up in sacrifice to the old heathen gods.

A ghostly chariot, drawn by white oxen, was also seen formerly driving down the stream to Schaffhausen, where it went thrice around the town. When this circuit took place from right

THE FALLS OF THE RHINE.

to left, it was considered an infallible sign of good fortune; but when it made the journey in an opposite direction, bad luck was sure to ensue.

In olden times, when nothing but a convent and boat-landing stood on the present site of the city of Schaffhausen, a nobleman once came down to the river to fish. Weary of his exertions, he finally fastened his skiff, and lying down in the bottom of it, fell asleep.

But while thus oblivious of all that was taking place, his vessel slipped its moorings, and drifting out into mid-current, was swept over the falls. The passenger was so sound asleep, however, that he did not even rouse when hurled down into the thundering abyss, and was greatly amazed on awakening to find his boat had drifted ashore far below the dreaded cataract.

In token of gratitude for this narrow escape, this nobleman is said to have founded the Benedictine abbey at Rheinau. on the very spot where his skiff drifted ashore after its perilous journey down the Rhine.[1]

A young fisherman, who had a similar experience, fatuously imagined that if his vessel went

[1] For other legends of Schaffhausen, etc., see the author's "Legends of the Rhine."

safely over the falls without being steered, it could not fail to do the same when guided by an experienced hand. He therefore loudly boasted that he was about to go over the cataract again, and in spite of all remonstrances on the part of friends and relatives, actually made the attempt.

The skiff, however, was soon caught in the whirling waters, and in spite of all the fisherman's efforts, dashed against the rocks. For one minute the horrified spectators saw the broken boat and clinging youth pause on the brink of the abyss, then they were swept over into the whirlpool, whence they never emerged ! Since then, on the anniversary of this foolhardy attempt, the ghost of the reckless youth can be seen drifting down the stream, and with a blood-curdling cry of despair it invariably plunges over into the vortex at the foot of the Rhine Falls.

WHEN noble knights still dwelt on the Randenberg, a pious maiden set out from there before dawn every morning to walk to the convent of All Saints at Schaffhausen, where it was her custom to attend early mass.

Her sole escort on this daily walk was a faithful stag, which patiently awaited her coming at the castle gates every morning. When it was very dark, this faithful animal walked lightly ahead of her, proudly carrying a flaming torch between its branching antlers, and it always waited at the city gates to accompany her home.

One day when the pious maiden and her attendant stag were nearing the city, they were suddenly attacked by wayside thieves. With a cry of terror, the maiden sped on as fast as her trembling limbs would carry her ; but when she came to the city gates she saw with terror that they were still shut. Knowing no human help could reach her in time to save her from the hands of the miscreants, she now had recourse to a short but fervent prayer, and the last words were scarcely uttered when an angel darted down from heaven, keys in hand, and led the maiden into the city, closing and locking the gates in the very face of the cruel highwaymen.

Ever since the pious maiden was thus miraculously saved by angelic intervention, that gate of Schaffhausen has been known as the Engelbrechtsthor, or the gate broken open by an angel.

WHERE the recently restored castle of Munot now stands, there was once an older building occupied by a noble lord, who set out for a pilgrimage to the Holy Land, leaving wife and children safe at home.

Those were the days of slow travel and no mail; so months became years without the Lady of Munot's receiving any tidings of her absent spouse. She therefore began to fear that he was dead, or that he had entirely forgotten wife and children at home. But such was not the case, for the knight, having surmounted many perils, was now very near home, and spurring on with all haste, in spite of the darkness, to see his family sooner.

Only a short stretch of wood, and the torrent of the Mühlenthal lay between him and his castle; but although the knight fancied he knew every inch of the ground, he soon lost his way. Instead of crossing the swollen stream at the usual place, he plunged into its waters at the most dangerous point, only to find a watery grave within sight and sound of home. One of his faithful retainers, however, managed to escape from the torrent, and sadly bore the sorrowful tidings to the poor widow.

When the Lady of Munot learned how her spouse had perished, she put on mourning which she never laid aside, and to prevent other belated travellers from meeting a similar fate, hung a silver bell in the castle tower and had it rung for an hour every night.

The mournful toll of this little bell at nightfall not only served to guide travellers safely through the forest, and keep the knight's memory green, but also reminded his former vassals to say a prayer for the rest of their dead master's soul.

LEGENDS OF ZÜRICH.

ZÜRICH, the old Roman Turicum, on either side of the Limmat at the point where it flows out of the green-hued lake, is the capital of the canton of the same name, and noted alike for the beauty of its situation and for its famous University.

In the days of the early Christian persecution, Felix and Regula, the patron saints of Zürich, were beheaded near this town. Strange to relate, though, immediately after the execution, both martyrs picked up their severed heads, tucked them under their arms, and stalked off to the spot where the minster now stands, where they wound up their marvellous performances by burying themselves comfortably! On the spot where they suffered martyrdom Charlemagne erected a memorial pillar, above which he hung a bell, saying that it could be rung by any one who had been wronged, and that they should receive immediate justice.

During one of his visits to Zürich, Charlemagne took up his abode in the Choristers'

House, and while he sat there at table one day he suddenly heard a loud peal from the bell of justice. He immediately despatched a servant to see what wrong had been done, and was greatly annoyed when the man reported that careful search had failed to reveal the presence of any living creature. A few moments later the bell rang again, but when the servant once more announced that no one was there, the emperor bade his guards hide near the pillar, and seize the miscreant who dared to pull the bell of justice in mere fun.

Before long the bell sounded a third time, and a few moments later the guards rushed into the emperor's presence with faces blanched with fear, to report that a snake had coiled itself around the pillar, and seizing the rope in its teeth, tugged until the bell rang forth loud and clear. The emperor immediately rose from table, saying he must see this phenomenon with his own eyes, and followed by all his court went down to the pillar. As he drew near, the snake came forward to meet him, and rising upon its coiled tail, bowed low before the monarch in evident recognition of his exalted station. Then, dropping down to the earth once more, it crept away, turning from time to time, and making signs as if to invite the emperor to follow. The serpent's actions were so eloquent that Charlemagne, understanding them, obediently followed it down to the edge of the water, where, parting the reeds, the snake showed him its nest, in which sat an enormous toad.

Charlemagne now bade his guards seize and kill the intruder, and when the snake had bowed its thanks and contentedly coiled itself around its eggs, he went back to his interrupted meal, loudly praising the bell by means of which even dumb animals could appeal for justice.

The next day, while the emperor again sat at dinner, the guards rushed in breathlessly to announce the coming of the strange snake. Charlemagne quickly bade them stand aside and not try to hinder the reptile, which now crawled into the room where he sat, climbed up on the table, did obeisance to the emperor, and delicately lifting the cover of his drinking-cup, dropped into it a jewel of fabulous price. Then, replacing the cover of the vessel, the snake bowed low again, and creeping down, left the cloister to return to its nest by the lake.

According to one version of this legend, Charlemagne set this precious stone in a ring which he gave to his wife, Frastrada.[1] Un-

---

[1] For other version, see the author's "Legends of the Rhine."

known to him, however, the stone had the magic power of fixing his affections upon its wearer. When the queen, therefore, thought she was about to die, she slipped the ring into her mouth to prevent its falling into the hands of some rival. For eighteen years Charlemagne refused to part with his wife's body, and carried it with him wherever he went. But at the end of that time his minister Turpin discovered the secret of his infatuation, and obtaining possession of the magic stone, soon saw all Charlemagne's affections fixed upon him.

As the emperor's devotion proved somewhat of a bore to the old minister, he tried to get rid of the spell by casting the ring into the mineral springs at Aix-la-Chapelle. While out hunting the next day, Charlemagne urged his steed to drink of that water, and when the animal hastily withdrew its foot and refused to approach the pool again, the emperor dismounted to investigate the cause.

Touching the imprint of the horse's hoof, Charlemagne discovered that the mud was very warm, for he was near the hottest of these thermal springs. While resting near that pool, he was seized with such an affection for the spot that he soon founded there his capital of Aix-la-Chapelle.

In memory of the horse which guided him

hither, the Cathedral was built in the shape of a horseshoe, and as Charlemagne could not endure the thought of ever leaving this enchanted neighbourhood, he left orders to bury him in the minster of Aix-la-Chapelle.

On the spot where Charlemagne's famous bell once hung, at Zürich, stands the Wasserkirche, which now contains a large library with valuable and interesting manuscripts. Charlemagne's great-grandson Louis II. often visited Zürich, where his two pious daughters induced him to build a convent and the Frauenmünster.

It is said that the place for these buildings was staked out by angel hands, and that the stakes were connected by a silken string of the finest make. This rope was hung above the altar of the new church, where it remained until the Reformation. It was then removed with many other relics, and served for years as ordinary bell-rope in a private house.

The king's daughters, who both became abbesses, long dwelt at Baldern Castle, whence, however, they went down to the Frauenmünster whenever the bell rang for prayers. They even attended the midnight services there, and when it was very dark a stately stag invariably walked before them carrying a flaming torch between its antlers.

At the foot of the southern slope of the Albis — a green mountain near Zürich — lies the little lake of Türl or the Türlersee. Tradition claims that this valley once belonged to the lords of Schnabelberg, whose castle stood on the height still bearing that name. They intrusted the care of their lands to an unprincipled steward who once induced a miser to sell his daughter for a piece of rich land down in the valley. This iniquitous bargain had no sooner been concluded than the inhuman father hastened down to view his new farm ; but while he was inspecting it, a fearful storm arose. Thunderbolts, repeatedly striking the mountain, detached great masses of stone, which, in falling, made a dam across the valley.

In a few moments the rain, pouring down the mountain side in swift torrents, filled all the hollow made by this dam, covering every inch of land the miser had received in exchange for his child. Terrified by this visitation from Heaven, the unjust steward not only let the maiden go unharmed, but paid a rich dower to the convent she entered, and mended his evil ways as much as he could.

Near the Lake of Türl once lived a lady named Kriemhild, who was jealous because her neighbours' lands were more productive than her own.   In hopes of ruining their crops, she bade a Salamancan student flood their fields.   The latter, scorning magic arts for so simple a task, dug a deep ditch, which, allowing the waters of the lake to escape, would accomplish his evil purpose just as well.

St. Verena, passing by there accidentally, discovered his purpose, and before he could complete his task whisked him and Kriemhild off to the Glarnisch in Glarus, where both are condemned to dig in the ice and snow until they have made plants bloom in the desolate spot still known as St, Verena's or Vreneli's garden. As for the ditch it is still to be seen, and in memory of Kriemhild's evil intentions it still bears her name.

Only a short railway journey from Zürich is the ancient castle of Kyburg, which rises between Winterthur and Frauenfeld.   It once belonged to a family of the same name, a side branch of the famous house of Welfs or Guelfs.   To account for this name, tradition relates that a Kyburg having married Irmentrude, Charlemagne's sister-in-law, went to live with her in a castle near Altorf.

One day, a poor woman came to this castle

begging for food, and sadly yet proudly exhibited triplets, whose recent arrival into the world
prevented her working as usual for her living.
The Countess of Kyburg, seeing these children,
sternly refused all help to the woman, declaring
no faithful wife had ever been known to bear so
many children at once, and that she would not
encourage vice in her lands by giving alms to
women of bad lives.

The virtuous peasant woman, justly offended at
this harsh speech, turned angrily away.   But she
paused a moment at the gate, to call Heaven to
prove that she had always been true to her marriage vows by giving the Countess twelve children at a birth.   The Countess paid little heed to
this curse, but many months later she was terrified by the simultaneous arrival of twelve sons,
all exactly alike, and all unmistakable Kyburgs.

Now it happened that her husband was away
when these babes came into the world, and the
Countess, fearing he might take the same view
of the affair as she had taken of the poor
woman's triplets, bade her faithful old nurse
drown eleven of the babes in a neighbouring
pond.   The nurse, for whom the Countess of
Kyburg's words were law, immediately bundled
eleven of the boys into her apron, and stealing
out of the castle by a postern gate, made her

way towards the pool. She had nearly reached it when she was suddenly confronted by her master just returning home, and he immediately inquired what she had in her apron, and what she was going to do.

The poor woman, hoping to shield her mistress, stammered that she was on her way to drown a litter of wolf cubs; then she tried to slip past him, but he insisted on seeing the cubs, and when she resisted, laid violent hands upon the apron she held so tightly together. A mere glimpse of its contents made him hotly demand a full explanation, and when posted about every detail of the affair, he bound the nurse over to secrecy, took charge of the boys, and had them carefully brought up, unknown to his wife, who fancied they were all dead.

For six years the Count of Kyburg kept this secret, but at the end of that time he gave a great banquet, to which he invited all his relatives and friends. In the middle of this meal, the eleven boys, richly dressed, were shown into the hall by his order. The guests all stared in amazement at these children, who were so exactly like one another, and like the supposedly only son of their host, that no one could doubt their parentage.

While they were still speechless, the Count

of Kyburg suddenly inquired, in terrible tones, what punishment should be awarded to the person who had tried to murder eleven such promising young Welfs (Wolves)? At these words the guilty Countess suddenly fainted, and the guests were informed of the part she had played. When she recovered her senses, her husband generously forgave her, but the children he had rescued were known ever after by the name their father gave them when he first introduced them to his friends.

King Louis II. of France is said to have promised one of the Welfs as much land as he could ride around in a golden wagon in one day. This Welf immediately decided to secure the boon by a subterfuge, since he could not get it otherwise.

By his orders, a tiny golden wagon was made, and sitting upon this toy, placed in a wagon to which were harnessed his quickest pacing oxen, he rode around a tract of land on either side of the Rhine, which included the site of Kyburg Castle. Thus he won the Kyburg estate where his three sons were born. In due time two of these became bishops, equally renowned for their learning and great piety.

One of them, in serving Mass at Easter, saw

a huge poisonous spider fall into the chalice. Loath to disturb the communion service, he swallowed the spider with the wine, and after Mass sat down to table, where, however, he refused to partake of any food. Exhausted by a long spell of fasting, he soon fell asleep, and his drowsy head rested on the table, while his breath passed softly between his parted lips. His friends, watching him, suddenly saw the spider—an emissary of Satan—creep out of his mouth and slink away, having been unable to injure so good a man.

The two bishops once sat in the castle, before a well-spread board, on the eve of a solemn fast-day. Although food and wine lay in plenty before them, they partook of them but sparingly, and were so absorbed in pious conversation that they remained there hour after hour, quite unmindful of the flight of time. The castle clock had just pealed forth the midnight hour, and the solemn fast had begun, when their secretary stepped into the hall to inquire whether they still had need of his services. This man, envious of their reputation, had long been jealous of them, and anxious to catch them tripping so he could publish the fact abroad. When he therefore beheld them seated before a huge roast of boar's flesh, with several bottles full of wine still before them, his eyes flashed with malicious pleasure. A moment later, however, he stood with lowered eyes and in subservient attitude before his superiors, who bade him go to rest, and, in the kindness of their hearts, gave him a big portion of meat and a bottle of wine to carry away with him.

The secretary meekly thanked the bishops, and took leave of them with apparent humility; but no sooner had he closed the door behind him, than he rushed off to a neighbouring convent, his heart dancing with fiendish glee. Rousing the brethren, he told them, with every mark of sanctimonious regret, that their shepherds were faithless, for they were even now, on a solemn fast-day, partaking of forbidden meat and drink!

He added that when they found themselves detected in this wrong-doing, they tried to silence him by giving him a portion of their viands, thus making him a partaker in their sin. In proof of this assertion, he produced the food they had given him, and the monks all crowded around, with long-drawn faces, to see and smell these evidences of their superiors' guilt.

To the secretary's surprise, however, they soon turned indignantly upon him, declaring

that the so-called boar's flesh was the fish served
on the monastery table every fast-day ; and the
rich wine nothing but the small beer which invariably accompanied it. The secretary protested wrathfully, but when he, too, examined
those articles carefully, he was forced to acknowledge the monks right, and to confess that Providence had worked a miracle to prevent two
absent-minded saints from inadvertently com-
mitting a grievous sin.

LEGENDS OF ZUG

THE Lake of Zug, the home of prehistoric lake-builders, is beautifully situated at the foot of the Rigi, and separated from the Lake of Lucerne by a narrow strip of land. At one end of this small sheet of water is the city of Zug, the capital of the canton of the same name, and at the other extremity, the pretty city of Arth, at the foot of the Rossberg.

This mountain is famous for its landslides, which have cost many lives and buried whole villages at its foot. The legend ascribes these cataclysms to the hard-heartedness of the people, who incurred the anger of the dwarfs by refusing them hospitality, as was the case at Roll on the Lake of Thun. The city of Zug has twice been undermined by the lake. The first time, in 1435, two whole streets sank down into the water; but while science attributes such accidents to perfectly natural causes, legend tries to account for them in a more poetic way.

In the centre of the lake, far down below the surface of the water, nixies and water-nymphs

are supposed to dwell in a marvellous palace all
hung with gleaming crystal stalactites, paved
with silver and gold, and brightly lighted by
the sparkle of precious stones encrusting its
walls. The dainty inhabitants of this sub-
aqueous palace seldom rise to the surface of
the lake, except at night, when they are seen
in the moonlight, dancing here and there over
the waves, floating gently ashore, or hovering
along grassy banks, where they love to spread
out their mist like veils.

These nymphs occasionally appear at village
dances, where they can be distinguished from
mortal maidens by their superior beauty, and
by the ever wet hem of their long white gowns.
One of these nymphs fell violently in love with
the handsome young son of a magistrate of Zug,
and besides meeting him at dances on the green,
held nightly trysts with him on the edge of the
lake.

The youth was deeply enamoured with the
dainty nymph, and when she rose out of the
waves one evening with reddened eyelids, he
insisted upon knowing the cause of her grief.
The sprite now told him that her father, having discovered her infatuation for a mere mortal,
had forbidden her to have any further intercourse with him, unless he were willing to

follow her down into her father's abode and live
with her there in happy wedlock. The young
man, on hearing this, vowed he would be only
too happy were such a course possible to him,
but gently explained that the element in which
she lived was not adapted to human lungs. The
nymph, however, declared such an obstacle could
easily be removed, and immediately proffered
a magic draught, which would enable him to
breathe in the water as easily as in the air. The
enamoured youth quickly seized the cup she
tendered, and after quaffing the crystal clear,
tasteless fluid it contained, sank with her down
into the depths of the lake.

Delighted with his new powers, and with the
wonders he saw on all sides, the youth was
very happy for a while, but homesickness finally
seized him in the crystal palace. When the
nymph tenderly inquired what was the matter,
he sadly confessed that he longed to see his
parents and friends once more, and that he
would never be entirely happy unless he could
attend divine service regularly in his parish
church.

At these words the nymph's sweet face darkened, but it was soon illumined again by a
brilliant idea which she vowed she would put
into immediate execution. That evening, for

the first time, she left her beloved, and stealing
into the sleeping city, replaced all the drinking
water in the houses of two streets by the same
magic fluid she had given to the youth. Then,
plunging into the lake again, she called all her
father's minions to her aid, and gently and
noiselessly undermined those houses. When
the people were sound asleep the next night, she
drew them softly down to the bottom of the lake.

On awakening in this new element, on the
morrow, they found all their surroundings un-
changed, and took up their life where they had
left it off when they went to sleep the night
before. The youth could now hold constant
intercourse with his former neighbours and
friends, attend service whenever he pleased,
and he and all the others are still as happy as
the day is long, for the magic draught has
endowed them with the immortality which all
water spirits enjoy.

When the waters are very clear, you can still
see the spire of the sunken church and the
gables of the old houses, and people gifted with
particularly keen eyes and lively imaginations
can detect the stir of busy life in the streets,
catch the sound of ringing bells, and the deep
solemn tones of an organ, gently accompanying
the chants of the sunken congregation.

ON the spot where the boundaries of Zürich, Zug, and Schwyz converge, stands the Hohe Rhonen, the goal of charming excursions; for from the top of this mountain one can enjoy a fine view of the lake, the Sentis, and the Toggenburg and Glarus mountains.

Part of the Hohe Rhonen consists of fine pastures, and a legend claims that a miser once tried to cheat a widow and several orphans out of their portion of this soil. To establish his claim to the pastures, the wicked man not only resorted to forgery, but as the judge still seemed doubtful of the justice of his claims, boldly volunteered to swear on the spot itself that it was rightfully his. The judge accepted this offer, and accompanied by plaintiff, defendant, and several witnesses, wended his way up the mountain to the disputed alp. Standing on a huge granite boulder which lay there, the miser took his oath, holding up three fingers as usual, and when the judge cried, " Woe upon thee, if thou swearest falsely ! " boldly added, " If I have committed perjury, may these fingers sink into this hard stone as easily as into water ! "

Saying these words, he thrust his fingers downward, and to his horror and dismay felt them sink into the stone up to the second joint ! But although they entered so easily, he could not dra.. them out again, and standing there, a convicted perjurer, had to confess his sin. He had scarcely ceased speaking, when he was hidden from sight by a dark cloud, a terrible cry was heard, and when the rock again became visible to the amazed spectators, the man had disappeared, carried off to Hades by the Devil. But the stone, with the imprint of his perjured digits, is still known as the Three Finger Stone, and remains there as a constant warning against falsehood and treachery.

Not very far from the Hohe Rhonen, but in the canton of Schwyz, stands the church of Einsiedlen, a famous place of pilgrimage ever since the ninth century. The legend claims that the spot is particularly holy because Our Lord once drank from the fountain with fourteen mouths, while journeying through the country to preach the gospel.

Besides, Meinrad, Count of Sulgen, having vowed to spend the rest of his life in prayer, came to this lovely valley long years ago. Here he built a little chapel to contain a wonder-working image of the Virgin, which he had received from one of the princess-abbesses of Zürich. Meinrad also built a small hut close by this chapel, and as this was generally called his hermitage (Einsiedelei), its name was given to the town which has since arisen on that spot.

Meinrad was known far and wide for his piety as well as for his charity, and all the gifts he received from strangers were immediately lavished upon the poor. Years were spent by the hermit in penance, prayer, and works of mercy, and when very old, the death angel suddenly appeared to him one day in the chapel, to announce that his end was near.

Meinrad, who had longed for Heaven for many a year, received this warning with solemn joy, and after returning thanks went out of the chapel, to feast his eyes once more upon the lovely landscape. While he sat near his hermitage, two tame ravens which he had brought up came to nestle in his lap, and he gently stroked them with his aged and trembling hands. While he sat there quietly, two robbers suddenly sprang out of the thicket, and exclaiming that they had come for the treasures accumulated during all these years, drove their daggers deep into his heart.

The old man fell to the ground lifeless, the ravens flew croaking away, and the thieves. picking up the corpse, threw it into the chapel, so as not to have it continually under their eyes while they made their search. With feverish haste they next turned over every article in the little hermitage, ripped open the straw pallet, peered into the depths of the one crock, and dug up the floor : but to their chagrin no treasure was forthcoming. Thinking the holy man might have concealed his wealth in the chapel, they now betook themselves thither; but no sooner had they crossed the threshold than they paused aghast, feeling their hair slowly rise up on end.

The chapel, which had been so dark a while ago, was now illumined by lights burning on the altar; the corpse was carefully laid out at its base, with tapers burning all around it, and close by stood the two crows, mounting solemn guard over their dead master. But when the murderers, recovering a little from their first surprise and terror, ventured to take a step forward, these faithful birds forsook their post, and so furiously attacked the intruders with beak and claws that they soon drove them out of the chapel.

Terrified by this attack, the robbers fled over the mountains to Zürich, and did not feel quite safe until seated in a little inn where they were wont to linger for hours. They were drinking hard, hoping to forget their recent uncanny experiences, when in through the open window suddenly flew two ravens which circled wildly around their heads, croaking loudly and threatening to pick out their eyes. The criminals, with a common impulse, ducked their heads, and groaning aloud, exclaimed : " Meinrad's watchers ! Meinrad's watchers ! "

These words, and the mysterious behaviour of the birds, which could not be driven away for some time, so aroused the suspicions of the city magistrates, that they sent both men to prison until they could ascertain whether Meinrad were still safe. That same evening, however, a traveller reported the murder of the hermit, whom he had found dead in the chapel. and when the judges summoned the prisoners they had to confess their crime. In punishment for slaying a hermit whom all revered like a saint, the murderers were first broken on the wheel and then burned at the stake.

A monastery was soon erected on the site of Meinrad's hermitage ; and since then a beautiful church, a fine abbey, and many inns and hotels have been built for the accommodation and edification of tourists and pilgrims who visit Einsiedlen in great numbers.

THURGAU

THE canton of Thurgau, bordering on the Lake of Constance, is less frequently visited by tourists than almost any other, because it consists principally of arable land and thriving manufacturing towns. It is not, however, without romantic interest ; but most of its legends are only slight variations of those already mentioned in connection with other places.

In the days of Charlemagne a Thurgau giant named Kisher joined the imperial forces, and went with them to fight against the Huns and Avars. Such was the size and strength of this warrior that he waded across every river, however deep, and when his horse hesitated to follow him, dragged it after him by its tail, crying, " Comrade, you must come along too ! "

In presence of the enemy this mighty giant remained unmoved, and placing himself at the head of the army, mowed down the foe as calmly and steadily as if he were cutting hay in his native country. The battle over, Kisher strung seven or eight of his victims on his lance,

and flinging it across his shoulder, tramped home
as coolly as if returning from a day's hunt with
his game. Such were his prowesses that Charlemagne declared that, as he was a host in himself, his name should be changed from Kisher to
Einheer, which means an army.

In going from Romanshorn to Constance, one
passes the village of Güttingen with its old
castle. The lords of this place, equally noted
for their wealth and avarice, had several other
castles, one of which stood so near the lake
that the waves constantly dashed against its
walls.

Once, when there was a great famine in the
land, the starving people, knowing their lords
had great quantities of food stored away in their
granaries, surrounded the castle and began to
clamour loudly for grain. The lords of Güttingen, who were living on the fat of the land
themselves, would not give anything to the poor,
and, weary of their importunate cries, determined to get rid of them once for all.

They therefore bade their hungry vassals assemble in an empty old barn, where they assured
them their pangs would soon be stilled. The
people, thinking their masters were about to
distribute food, thronged into this place ; but

when it was full, almost to overflowing, the cruel lords of Güttingen bade their servants close the doors and set fire to the building. When the bright flames rose all around them, the poor victims loudly begged for mercy ; yet although their pitiful cries would have touched any one else, the lords of Güttingen quietly sat there on their steeds, and laughed aloud when one of them sarcastically cried, " Just hear those mice squeak ! "

Before long the roof fell in and the clamours ceased ; but from the smoking ruins suddenly came hosts of mice, which, running straight to the Güttingen castles, devoured everything they could find.   The lords themselves, terrified at the sight of these pests, fled to their Wasserburg, or Castle in the Water.   But the mice pursued them there too, and having disposed of everything else, pounced upon them. In a few moments heaps of clean picked bones were all that was left of these heartless lords, whose castle shortly afterwards sank into the lake.   There its ruins can be seen when the water is very low, and some people claim you can still hear mice gnawing the bones of those cruel men if you listen very attentively.[1]

[1] For similar legends of Bingen and others of this section, see the author's "Legends of the Rhine."

A Count of Seeheim eloped with a maiden of Kyburg because her father objected to their union. The lovers, dreading the Count of Kyburg's wrath, placed themselves immediately under the protection of the Abbot of Reichenau, who promised to aid and watch over them, and pronounced their nuptial benediction.

The bride, having a fortune of her own, soon built a castle near the boundary of her father's land, carefully providing it with strong walls so that he could not molest her or her beloved spouse. For some time after the two families lived on a war footing, but in course of time a complete reconciliation took place.

In memory of this feud and of its happy termination, the town which rose around the new castle received the name of Frauenfeld, and the coat of arms of that city still bears the effigy of the faithful woman. She is represented controlling a lion, which fierce animal is intended to represent the race from which she sprang, and whose wrath she successfully defied and subdued.

ST. GALL AND APPENZELL

ST. GALL, capital of the canton of the same name, which entirely surrounds that of Appenzell, is noted for the famous abbey founded in 614 by St. Gallus, an Irish monk. He had come into this unsettled region to preach the gospel, and when his disciple Hiltiboldus urged that they would be exposed to the attacks of the bears, wolves, and boars, quietly answered, " If God is with us, who can be against us ? "

The snakes which had infested that region departed for good and all at the saint's command, and his disciple soon discovered that even the wild beasts of the forest stood in awe of so holy a man. One evening, while Gallus was praying at the foot of a rustic cross, a bear came down the mountain to devour his provisions. St. Gallus, perceiving the theft, quietly bade the bear earn the food he had eaten, by bringing wood to keep up his fire. The crestfallen Bruin humbly fulfilled this penance, and when the saint told him henceforth to remain on the heights, never ventured down into the valley again.

One day Gallus's disciple discovered an apple-tree far up the mountain, and climbing up shook down some fruit to carry home to his master. But when he slid to the ground again, he was dismayed to find a huge bear on the other side of the tree greedily munching the fallen apples. The disciple's first impulse was to flee, but remembering that his master was fond of fruit, he determined to secure some for him. Taking his staff, therefore, he scratched deep marks at right angles with the tree, and then gravely informed the bear that while he was welcome to the apples on his side of the line, those which fell on the other were reserved for St. Gallus. Strange to relate, the bear understood this speech, and as long as the apples lasted never ventured to touch one on the saint's side of the line, although he devoured all those on his own!

The cell and cross of St. Gallus were the nucleus of a monastery and school, which for several centuries had no rival in Europe. Kings and emperors were wont to visit it, and the abbey, enriched by their gifts and concessions, daily increased in importance and wealth.

Within the walls of this edifice dwelt men noted for their learning, and countless scribes spent their lives there, patiently copying and illuminating manuscripts which, but for their

efforts, might have been lost to mankind. Some
of these manuscripts still remain in the abbey
library ; among others, a thirteenth century
copy of the Niebelungenlied, Germany's famous
epic.   Innumerable scholars visited the school
and abbey at St. Gall, which is said to have
been the scene of a comical encounter between
the abbot and Charlemagne, almost an exact
counterpart of the story of King John and the
Archbishop of Canterbury.[1]

The old monastery life so ably depicted in
" Ekkehard," by Von Scheffel, with its descrip-
tions of the herdsmen and hermit on the Sentis,
have surrounded that region with a halo of romance for all who have enjoyed the perusal of
the book.

THE Sentis, with its cap of snow, is the highest mountain in Appenzell, and the goal for
travellers who wish to make a whey cure or to
enjoy an excursion to its summit.   From the
top of this mountain the view embraces the Lake
of Constance, southern Germany, the Tyrolean
Mountains, and the Alps in Glarus and Bern.
All the way up are various pastures with their
low châlets, where butter and cheese are constantly made and carried down the steep paths

[1] See the author's " Legends of the Rhine."

for consumption in the valleys. The Sentis, like all other mountains where cattle go to pasture, is supposed to be haunted by mountain-folk, who, when well treated, are always helpful to mortals.

The Devil, too, plays his part in the Sentis legends, for one of them claims that a lazy herdsman once called upon him to take his cattle, so that he need no longer run after them when they strayed into dangerous places. The words were no sooner uttered than a hurricane swept down the mountain, and the terrified peasant saw Satan, riding on the wind, drive his cows over the edge of the abyss. In sudden repentance he made a sign of the cross, fell on his knees, and cried that he had sinned grievously. At those words the wind ceased, the Devil vanished; but ever since then the pasture, which had been known as the Glücksalp, or Lucky Alp, has been called Im Fehlen, or In Sin.

ANOTHER legend claims that the Devil once came striding across northern Switzerland with a huge bag slung over his shoulder. In this sack he had packed away a large number of houses, together with their inhabitants, and was carrying them away with the intention of removing them for ever from Swiss soil. While taking a leap over the Sentis, however, he burst a hole in his bag, and the houses all tumbled down in Appenzell, where they still stand in irregular groups, just as they fell.

The same story which is told of the Alphorn at Meiringen is also told of the heights near the much frequented baths of Ragatz, in the southern part of the canton of St. Gall. Not very far from this resort, and on the same wild stream, the Tamina, are the no less noted baths of Pfäfers, and farther up the gorge an ancient abbey of the same name, to which legend ascribes the following origin : —

In the beginning of the eighth century St. Pirminius and his disciple Adalbert preached the gospel in the eastern part of Switzerland. Their efforts were rewarded with such success that they determined to build a chapel and monastery in this part of the country. Wishing to secure the Pope's consent and blessing for this undertaking, Pirminius set out for Rome, bidding Adalbert in the meantime select a suitable site and begin clearing ground.

After much search Adalbert decided upon a lovely sheltered valley, where the sun shone brightly, where grass and fruit-trees were abundant, and where limpid waters flowed gently through meadows and forests. He and his converts now began felling trees, but while doing so Adalbert's axe suddenly slipped, inflicting a deep wound in his sandalled foot. The blood gushed forth, staining the chips around, and while all were trying to check its flow, a white dove suddenly alighted near them, and catching up a gory chip, flew off to a neighbouring tree. At the same moment Adalbert's blood stopped running, the wound closed, and in a moment he felt no more pain.

This miraculous cure seemed to all connected in some way with the dove; so when the bird flew slowly away with the chip, Adalbert determined to follow it. Flitting from tree to tree and from rock to rock, the dove entered the cold and dark Tamina gorge, and penetrating ever farther, finally perched on a sombre pine, and dropped the bloody chip at its foot. Returning to his companions, Adalbert now told them he must await Pirminius' return, and relate these marvels to him so that he might interpret them if he could.

When the saint came back from Rome and learned what had happened, he immediately cried that Providence had sent them a sign, wishing them to build a church and abbey on the spot where the dove had dropped the bloody chip.

He added that such a wild, desolate region was more fitted to encourage a life of constant penance, labour, and prayer than the valley flowing with milk and honey first chosen by Adalbert. By his orders the Abbey of Pfäfers was begun, and to this day its seal bears a white dove carrying a bloody chip in its beak, in memory of the miracle to which it owes its location.

GLARUS AND GRISONS.

NEAR the city of Chur or Coire, and at the
foot of the majestic Calanda, are the ruins
of several castles, among others that of Haldenstein. Not very far from its crumbling walls is
a fine spring of clear water, where people claim a
charming vision was often seen. Dressed in a
long white gown which fell in classic folds to her
feet, this lovely maiden was wont to linger on
the sunniest spot by the edge of the spring, dab-
bling her hands in its cool waters. A hunter once
came to this place, saw the beautiful maiden,
and heard her weeping softly. He immediately
drew near and looked at her so compassionately
that she told him if he would only hold her hand
and not let it go until she bade him, he would
release her from the baleful spell which caused
her tears.

The young man unhesitatingly took her slender white hand between his own sunburned
palms, but started at finding it as cold as ice.
While he held it tight, trying to communicate a
little of his own warmth to the chilled fingers,

a tiny old man came out of the castle and silently offered him a diamond basket full of gold. Although he could easily have secured this treasure by stretching out one hand, the young huntsman continued the task he had voluntarily undertaken, and was soon rewarded by feeling a little warmth steal into the slender hand he held so firmly. At the same time the girl's sad eyes beamed with pleasure, a slight flush stole into her pallid cheeks, and looking up at him, she joyfully exclaimed, —

" I see I was not mistaken. You have proved trustworthy; so you may now let go my hand, and take that basket as a token of my gratitude."

The maiden softly drew her hand from his, gave him the treasure, and vanished with a seraphic smile.

Since then the White Lady of Haldenstein has never been seen by mortals, but the spring over which she mounted guard became known far and wide for its curative properties. These lasted for many a year; but although the spring still flows as clear as ever, it is said to have now lost all its healing powers.

On the way from Coire to Castiel one passes the awful Tobel, where a huge dragon once took up its abode. Such were the ravages it made in that region that the people of Castiel, Calfriesen, and Lüen solemnly pledged themselves to provide it with a human victim every year on condition that the monster left them unmolested the rest of the time.

The dragon in the Castieltobel agreed to this arrangement, and the yearly victim was chosen by lot from each of the villages in turn. Now it came to pass that a tall, muscular stranger soon came to settle there with his only daughter, and when the lot fell upon her, he boldly declared he would accompany her to the monster's den, and slay it or perish with her.

Leading the maiden by one hand, and holding his trusty sword tight in the other, the brave man advanced cautiously, followed at a safe distance by all the people, who wished to witness his encounter with the dragon. They did not have to wait long, for, ravenous after a whole year's fast, the monster rushed eagerly forward to swallow its prey. It had already opened wide its capacious jaws, when the desperate father rushed toward it, thrust his sharp blade right into its throat, and inflicted such a severe wound that the dragon expired a moment later.

Overcome with joy at having saved his beloved daughter, the father now fell on his knees, and raising his hands to Heaven, gave solemn thanks for her preservation. While he was in that attitude, a drop of dragon-blood fell from his sword upon his head, and such was the deadly nature of the venom that it instantly killed him. The village people were so grateful to him for delivering them from this dragon, however, that they generously provided for his daughter, and erected a church on the very spot where he had breathed his last.

About half-way between Castiel and Davos is the village of Arosa, where grows a fine tree from beneath whose roots gushes a living spring. According to popular superstition, lucky people can find a golden key in the hollow whence this water flows from the ground. As soon as secured, one suddenly perceives a passage-way barred by an iron door, which can only be opened by means of this golden key.

A herdsman, who once came to refresh himself at this spring, discovered this key by great good fortune. and boldly opening the locked door, found himself in a vast cave. There a dwarf bade him choose between a heap of gold and diamonds, which would make him the wealthiest man in the country; a golden cow-bell which would assure him the possession of the finest cattle for miles around; or a lovely girl, whose eyes were fixed imploringly upon him, and who softly whispered that he would find true happiness only with her.

The young man hesitated, but as he had a passion for fine cows, he finally left the cave with the golden bell. He felt so weary upon leaving this place, however, that he lay down to rest a moment near the spring, and soon fell asleep. When he awoke, the magic key had vanished, and he might have believed the whole adventure a mere dream, had not the golden bell still lain beside him.

On returning to his post, he found his herd miraculously increased, and all his cows were so handsome that his neighbours soon became jealous of him, and refused to have anything more to do with him. The young herdsman, therefore, left alone with his cattle, often regretted he had not chosen an intelligent companion to share his solitude; but although he frequently tried to find the golden key again, and thus secure the fair maid he had once seen, it was all in vain. Within a year from that time, he lost all his fine cattle, because he brooded continually over his loneliness instead of taking care of them, and before long he committed suicide by flinging himself down from the top of one of the sharp peaks near there.

EAST of Coire and south of the lovely Prätigau, is Davos Platz, so charmingly located near the top of a pass, where it is well sheltered from the northeast winds. Besides its interest as a health resort visited by many noted people, and the beautiful scenery and healthful climate, this place derives additional charms from its legends. On the western slope of the Davos Schwartzhorn, for instance, there is a place generally known as the Dead Alp. Not a shrub or blade of grass is seen there now; so it offers a striking contrast to the many other fine pastures in that vicinity.

In olden days this desolate spot was the finest grazing-ground for miles around, for it was then thickly covered with heavy grass, and watered by springs of the freshest water. At one time the land belonged to a rich young dairy maid, who came down into the valley one fine Sunday afternoon to dance on the village green. She had so many partners, and so thoroughly enjoyed herself with them, that she did not want to go home, although she knew that it was time to milk the cows. Duty warned her to return; but the delights of dancing proved so tempting that she determined to linger, and tried to silence the voice of conscience by recklessly cursing both pasture and kine.

This malediction had scarcely left her lips, when her fruitful alp was turned into a desert, her cows all vanished, and she suddenly found herself deprived of all the worldly goods she had so little known how to appreciate!

OTHER Davos herdsmen, as pleasure-loving as she, once cursed the Icelandic moss or Cyprian herb which was then so rich in milk-producing qualities that they had to milk their cows several times a day. No sooner was the curse uttered than the luscious herb dried up, and ever since then it has been the poorest sort of fodder, which no animal will eat as long as something else can be found to satisfy its hunger.

NOT very far from the Dead Alp, you can see, summer and winter, a broad field of snow, far below the usual snow-line. This, too, was once a luxuriant pasture, where herdsmen were kept very busy tending their cows, and making butter and cheese from the milk they gave in such profusion.

The owner of this alp was so good and generous that the poor were in the habit of going up there for food whenever they were hungry, and there was much wailing among them when

he grew ill and died, and they heard the pasture
now belonged to an avaricious man. They soon
found the new proprietor was even worse than
they expected, for he was very cruel too, and
drove all beggars away with curses and hard
blows.

A poor but numerous family, travelling
through the country, climbed up these heights
one cold and foggy day, to beg for the food and
shelter no one else could have denied them.
But when they drew near the châlet, cross dogs
rushed out to meet them, barking, snarling, and
showing their teeth in the fiercest way. The
poor people nevertheless made their way to the
door, where they stood, humble suppliants, while
the oldest among them described their pitiful
plight and asked for aid.

The hard-hearted herdsman would not listen
to him, however, roughly bade him begone with
all his family, and seeing he did not immediately
obey, called out to his men to drive the beggars
away. This order was only too promptly
obeyed. The rough servants rushed out, and
falling upon the poor family, lashed them with
their long whips, threw stones at them, and
laughed with uproarious glee when their fierce
dogs began to chase the beggars down the
mountain.

Besides several old people, there were weak women and puny little children among these poor fugitives ; still these cruel men felt no respect for age or sex, and merely urged on their dogs worse than ever. Their inhumanity proved too much for an old man, who, as he tottered last down the path, with torn garments and bleeding limbs, suddenly turned around and cursed their alp, wishing it might soon be hidden beneath a covering of snow that might rest upon it for ever.

That wish was fulfilled the self-same night, for huge masses of snow and ice fell down upon the pasture, transforming it into a wintry waste, which well deserves its name, the Cursed Alp. Since then, whenever a storm rages, or whenever fog envelops the mountain, the buried herdsmen rise from their shroud of snow, and one can again hear them snapping their whips, exciting their dogs, and hotly pursuing ghosts of beggars whom they are condemned to chase for ever in punishment for their sins.

In the centre of the Grisons arises a reddish peak known as the Rothhorn, which towers above all the other heights around it, and from whence a fine view can be enjoyed.

It is said that the people of Plurs once exploited the gold mines in this mountain, and thus became very rich. All this prosperity was not owing to their exertions alone, but due mainly to the fact that they had won the good graces of the gnomes, who, at noon every day, poured a canful of liquid gold down into a vein which they could easily reach.

Unfortunately, the people of Plurs did not make a wise use of this wealth, but drank, gambled, and led vicious lives. This fact so incensed their former friends, the mountain spirits, that they slyly loosened great masses of stones and dirt, and hurled them down upon the city one dark night in 1618.

Only one of the inhabitants, a pack-driver, escaped from general destruction. He had arrived in the village late, intending to tarry there overnight, but his leading mule refused to stop at the inn, and passing on was dutifully followed by all the rest, although the driver tried to stop them. Three times this man drove his train back to the inn, but three times they passed by, and the pack-driver had to follow.

When they had gone some distance from the city for the third and last time, the man suddenly heard a terrible noise, and, looking behind him, witnessed the landslide and the total destruction of the once prosperous little city.

THE Engadine Valley, noted for its bracing climate, is rather bleak, for, according to a popular saying, it boasts nine months of winter and three of cold.

In the seventh century St. Florinus with one disciple came to Rémus, in the northern part of this valley, to preach the gospel. Feeling very weak and ill one day, the saint bade his faithful companion beg some wine at a neighbouring castle to restore his failing strength.

The disciple obeyed, and having secured a crockful, slowly wended his way home. He soon met a poor woman weeping bitterly, and inquiring the cause of her sorrow, learned that her husband had been very ill, and that she had no money to buy the wine he needed to restore his strength. Touched by her tears, the disciple poured all he had received into the vessel she held, and then went back to the castle to beg for more. But the people up there, having seen him give the wine to the poor woman, now reproved him harshly, and sent him empty-handed away. The disciple departed sadly, regretting his generous deed; and, fearing to present himself before his master with an empty crock, he filled it with water at a wayside spring. As soon as St. Florinus saw him standing at his bedside, he reached up eagerly, seized the crock, and took a long deep draught. The disciple, who fully expected an exclamation of bitter disappointment, was dumfounded to hear the saint declare he had never tasted such good and strengthening wine ; and, when invited to try it also, he discovered that the miracle of Cana had been repeated, for the Lord had again turned water into wine. This transformation took place, as long as the saint needed a tonic ; but when he was quite well, the crock was found to contain nothing but water as before.

THE people of the Engadine valley are very simple indeed ; so simple that a legend claims they were often cheated, and never could decide what it was best to do.   A traveller, hearing the people of Sils complain, mischievously suggested that they ought to buy a little wisdom, and when they seriously inquired what it was and where it could be procured, he gravely informed them that it was a precious herb, purchasable only in Venice.

The people, believing him implicitly, took up a collection and sent an emissary to Italy to buy the rare plant.   After a long painful journey, this man came home, having purchased from a charlatan the only sprout of the herb of wisdom

still to be had in that city. The people all
crowded eagerly around their emissary to see
and admire the wonderful herb, compared it ex-
haustively with those which grew around them,
and although they could perceive but little difference, planted it carefully on their village green.
But, while they were indulging in a great jollifi-
cation to celebrate the advent of wisdom among
them, an old donkey came straying along, and
before they could prevent it, ate up the precious
plant !

Since then, the people of Sils have never been
able to secure another specimen, and it is said
they still grievously mourn their great loss.

THE scene of the above legend is located in
the Upper Engadine or Inn Valley, south of
the much frequented towns of St. Moritz and
Pontresina.

From there, you can see the dazzling snow
top of the Bernina, a high mountain between
Switzerland and Italy, with a much travelled
pass leading from the Engadine to the Valteline
Valley. Journeying from Poschiavo over the
Bernina, one passes a desolate spot formerly
occupied by the small town of Zarera. The
inhabitants of that place are said to have
taken advantage of their position on the high-

way between Italy and Switzerland, to extort
money from all the pack-drivers and travellers who passed through there. In fact, they
enriched themselves by such unlawful and ques-
tionable means that they finally incurred the
wrath of Heaven. One night, when the moon
was partly veiled by shifting clouds, a maiden
dressed in white rode slowly around their town
on a snowy palfrey, calling to them to repent
while it was still time. But this admonition fell
upon ears that would not hear, and the predicted
retribution soon came. Dark clouds gathered
around the top of the mountain, vivid flashes of
lightning zigzagged through the ever-increasing
gloom, and soon the rain came down in such
torrents that rocks and trees were swept down
the mountain like pebbles and chips. In a few
minutes the once prosperous town of Zarera
was completely annihilated, and only the frag-
ments of ruined houses could still be detected
here and there. All the people perished in this
flood, with the exception of a mother and
daughter, noted for their piety, who dwelt at
some distance from the wicked town.

These two women had been very busy that
day, doing their semi-annual baking; for, like
most of the people around there, they made
bread only twice a year. In spite of the serious

work on hand, they prayed as long and read their Bible as diligently as usual, and even while setting the bread to rise, commented reverently upon the teachings contained in Our Lord's mentions of leaven and flour.

From time to time one or the other gazed out into the garden, where chestnut-trees three hundred years old overshadowed their little house. The southern exposure and the protection afforded by the mountain against the cold winds from the north and east, made their peach and apricot trees bloom already in February, allowed fresh figs to grow close at hand, and made their vines as productive as those in the Valteline. The two women were very grateful for all these blessings, and would have been perfectly happy with their lot, had they not sorely missed their husband and father, who had died three years before.

While taking the huge loaves of sweet-smelling fresh bread out of the oven, they thrice heard the melancholy, wailing note of the storm bird, but they were so absorbed in their occupations that they paid no heed to it, until the tempest fairly broke over their heads and the rain began to fall with violence.

All through that awful storm, which wrecked the town of Zarera, they knelt in prayer, and when morning came and the downpour ceased, they found their garden transformed into a stony waste, and all their trees uprooted and swept down into the valley.

In spite of the losses which suddenly deprived them of their means of existence, these two women returned fervent thanks for their preservation, and seeing that their house was now unsafe, and that it would be useless to remain on the mountain, they picked up their few remaining possessions, and wended their way down into the valley. There they soon found shelter, and by dint of hard work finally managed to retrieve their shattered fortunes ; but, as long as they lived, they both remembered the awful storm in which they would surely have perished had it not been for the hand of God stretched out in protection over them.

FOLLOWING the Rhine's devious course toward its source in the St. Gothard mountain, we come to the junction of two branches of this stream at Disentis.[1] Here stands an abbey, dating from the seventh century, when its monks served as missionaries to the people around them.

The heathen from the banks of Lake Con-

---

[1] For other data, see the author's "Legends of the Rhine."

stance once made a raid down this valley, and visiting every castle, church, convent, and hut, destroyed almost everything they could not carry away. Laden with booty, they were slowly making their way north again, when they were surprised at Disentis by the exasperated Swiss. The latter there attacked the heathen with such fury that all those who were not killed were only too glad to seek safety in precipitate flight.

The brave Swiss were so weary, when the battle was over, and so parched with thirst, that they longed for a drink. As there was no spring near by, and as their extreme exhaustion would not permit their going in search of one, their venerable old leader made a short but fervent prayer, and then thrust his sword into the ground up to the very hilt. When he slowly drew it out again a moment later, a strong jet of water shot straight up into the air, and falling down again on the rocky soil, soon formed a pool and brook where all could drink. This spring still flows as freely as ever, and its limpid waters possess medicinal properties which have since attracted many visitors to this picturesque spot.

THE line between Glarus and Grisons was long undetermined, so the shepherds from either

canton often indulged in raids and cattle-steal-
ing, which not infrequently resulted in violence
and bloodshed.

Once the men of Glarus suddenly came over
the border, and noiselessly surrounding a large
pasture, drove away all the cows, after tumbling
the herdsmen head first into the great kettles
of boiling milk where they were busy making
cheese. Only one of these men managed to
escape death by hiding in the hay. As soon
as the raiders vanished, he determined to sound
the alarm. Taking his horn, he therefore
climbed up into a pine-tree, just above the
great Flimser Rock, and calling through this
instrument with all his might, told his beloved
Trubina, who dwelt on another alp, of the mis-
fortune which had occurred. The strain was
such, however, that the unhappy youth burst
a blood-vessel, and sank dying from the top of
the tree. His life blood ran in a thin stream
over the great rock, where it made an indelible red streak, which can still be seen, and
which serves to remind people of his heroic
deed.

The timely warning he had given enabled
Trubina to start a party of Grisons herdsmen
after the cattle, which they followed down the
mountain to the village of Flims. By careful

reconnoitring, they soon ascertained that the cows had been turned into an enclosed orchard, just beside the inn where the raiders were celebrating their capture in the most convivial way.

Stealing unseen into this orchard, the Grisons men slyly fastened all the cow-bells to one steer, which they left in the enclosure, while they noiselessly drove all the rest of the herd home. The revellers, hearing the constant tinkle of cowbells, deemed their prizes quite safe, and were therefore greatly surprised and chagrined, when after their carousal they found only one bull calf in the enclosure, and saw how cleverly they had been duped.

On the frontier between Glarus and Uri, and not far from the Klausen Pass, where the great Boundary Race took place, rises a majestic glacier known as the Claridenalp. The people around there claim that this mountain was once fine pasture-land up to the very top, where a small ice-cap served to feed the many streams trickling down through the rich alps into the valley.

Most of the grazing on the Claridenalp once belonged to a young herdsman, who, although he revelled in plenty, cruelly let his old parents starve in the valley below him. This young man was, however, lavish enough when it suited him to be so, for he daily sent rich presents to his sweetheart, who, on the whole, was as selfish and heartless as he.

Finding separation from her unendurable, the young herdsman finally begged her to come up and spend the summer with him in his fine chålet, and receiving a favourable answer, immediately began elaborate preparations for her reception. His cows were groomed until they shone, and decked with bright ribbons and gar-lands of flowers; his larder stocked with every dainty he could secure, and lest his beloved should bruise her tender feet against a stone, or soil her dainty apparel in walking near the chålet, he paved the space all around it with fine rich cheeses, thus making a soft and smooth, if rather costly floor.

Meeting his sweetheart part way down the mountain, the herdsman joyfully escorted her to the chålet, where she duly admired all his ar-rangements, and encouraged his extravagance by throwing butter into the fire to keep up a bright flame. The revelry up in the chålet grew more fast and furious hour after hour, and the lovers feasted and sang, while the poor parents, faint from lack of food, lay shivering on their hard pallets down in the valley.

A burst of loud music floating down from the mountain finally roused the old father from his torpor. Sitting up in bed, he then shook his emaciated fist in the direction of the châlet, and solemnly cursed his unnatural son.

That night, an awful storm swept down the mountain, and when morning broke, the people in the valley saw that the Claridenalp had been transformed overnight into the glacier which you now see. Pasture and cattle, herdsman and sweetheart had all vanished, but the spirits of the lovers are said to haunt the site of their mad revelry.

Similar stories, with trifling variations, are told of many other snow mountains in Switzerland. The Plan Nevé, for instance, is said to have become a waste because a herdsman ill-treated his old mother. But the Blümelisalp, once the possession of a rich dairymaid, who built a staircase of cheeses from valley to châlet so she could more easily trip down to the weekly dances, was transformed into the present glacier, because she cruelly gave an aged beggar a drink of milk in which she maliciously stirred some rennet. The milk, turning suddenly into a hard lump of cheese in the poor woman's stomach, caused her such intolerable suffering that she cursed the cruel giver.

Since then, the alp, once thickly strewn with the many delicate Alpine flowers which gave it its name, has been almost inaccessible. But countless mortals constantly admire it from a distance, and breathlessly watch it flush at sunset, or glitter in all its icy splendour beneath the silvery rays of the full moon.

HELVETIA boasts of many other legends connected with nearly every part of her soil; but as they are mostly repetitions of those already quoted they are purposely omitted here. The samples of Swiss folklore already supplied will enable travellers to gain some idea of the old-time village tales which have cast their glamour over " the playground of Europe." These crude yet often poetical imaginings lend additional charms to scenery which rises before our mental vision whenever we hear or see the magic word " Switzerland."

Index